Between Hope & Tragedy

USA TODAY BESTSELLING AUTHOR

Yolanda Olson

Blurb

It all started with one mistake.

But that's what life is, isn't it?

One mistake after the other, hoping that one day, things will finally go right for a change.

I left when I got the chance.

I thought it would make everything okay.

But sometimes, things go awry and we all have to go back to the places that hurt us the most.

I should have expected it.

After all, everything can't be perfect forever.

One

Not everything in this world is as beautiful as it seems. A drop of dew sitting on the freshly-cut morning grass can hold a deadly bacteria invisible to the human eye. The stray cat that goes by my house every morning—with its lovely gray and white stripes—is feral and full of disease. The warmth of the afternoon sun that shines so lovingly on the world infiltrates the skin with cancerous cells, building up and waiting for the moment to strike.

But, like everyone else, I chose to ignore the danger hiding in everyday things and continued living as though nothing were wrong. I always thought that nothing could hurt me, because I was the flame, and as such, I couldn't be burned. Because I was a realist, I was waiting for the theoretical bucket of ice-cold water to be thrown over my head. I was waiting for the exact moment where I would be able to pinpoint every heartbreak, every sorrow I had experienced. come crashing down on me all at once.

I was sitting with my eyes closed, on a swing in the park, a few blocks away from my house. It was one of my favorite things to do because it gave me a chance to think. I never had a particular thought that I wanted to nail down, just a bunch of random things that would go through my head, and this was my place to let them flow freely. It was also my place to be alone because most people seemed to stay away from this here.

Just as I was slipping into my thought zone, I heard sounds of children laughing, and the pounding of racing footsteps.

I opened my eyes and looked at the slide curiously. There was a little girl with curly blonde hair climbing the ladder, while two older boys were following closely behind her. I smiled when she squealed happily as she went down the slide with her hands in the air. She couldn't have been more than five years old and her excitement at something so simple was enough to warm even my cold heart.

It also took me back to a memory of when I was fourteen years old. I turned my face away from the children and pushed the tip of my foot against the dirt, causing the swing to move back. With a sigh, I looked over at the man I assumed was their father who was reading a newspaper at the lone, wooden bench while the children played, and thought of another beautifully imperfect thing in the world.

Scars. They should be something to tell a proud story of survival, but the one I had—it told a story of guilt, depression, and loss. And while the scar may have healed nicely, the feelings I had when I got it never did.

My tale of woe happened when I was fourteen years old. I had stupidly fallen in love with my thirty-eight-year-old history teacher, Mr. Spears, and ended up falling pregnant. Since I refused to tell my parents who the father was, they made me give my child up for adoption. I never even got the chance to find out if it was a boy or a girl, to hold them, or to see if they looked like me or him. Once I had my cesarean, my baby got whisked away and I was left crying in the hospital room alone.

It was on the third night in the hospital that I started to watch the light fade from the beauty in the world, and it was around that same time I decided to harden myself toward any form of emotion ever again. I spent the next few years in my parents' home, going to school, trying to accept the fact that my history teacher had decided that I didn't exist to him anymore, and finally graduated as a sad, broken teenager. Now at twenty-eight years old, I was a full-blown adult living on my own and keeping to myself.

Days were normally easy for me, functioning like I had never known heartache; because I always forced it away. But seeing happy, carefree children always made me sad. It always made me wonder if my child was loved and felt more wanted than I ever did. Praying they wouldn't make the same mistakes I had, and that they had a shot at a normal life. Hoping that maybe they thought about me as much as I would think about them at times.

None of it really mattered, because they were away from me, so I knew that their chances of being a normal human being were exponentially better than if I had them. Still, I wouldn't go many days without thinking about them.

"Why are you thad?" a little voice lisped next to me.

I glanced to my left and smiled, blinking back tears I didn't even know had been forming. It was the little blonde girl, and she was looking at me curiously as she struggled to get into the swing next to me.

"Because it's the only way I know how to be," I responded with a shrug before I hopped off my swing and left the little blonde girl staring after me, with the curiosity only a child could achieve.

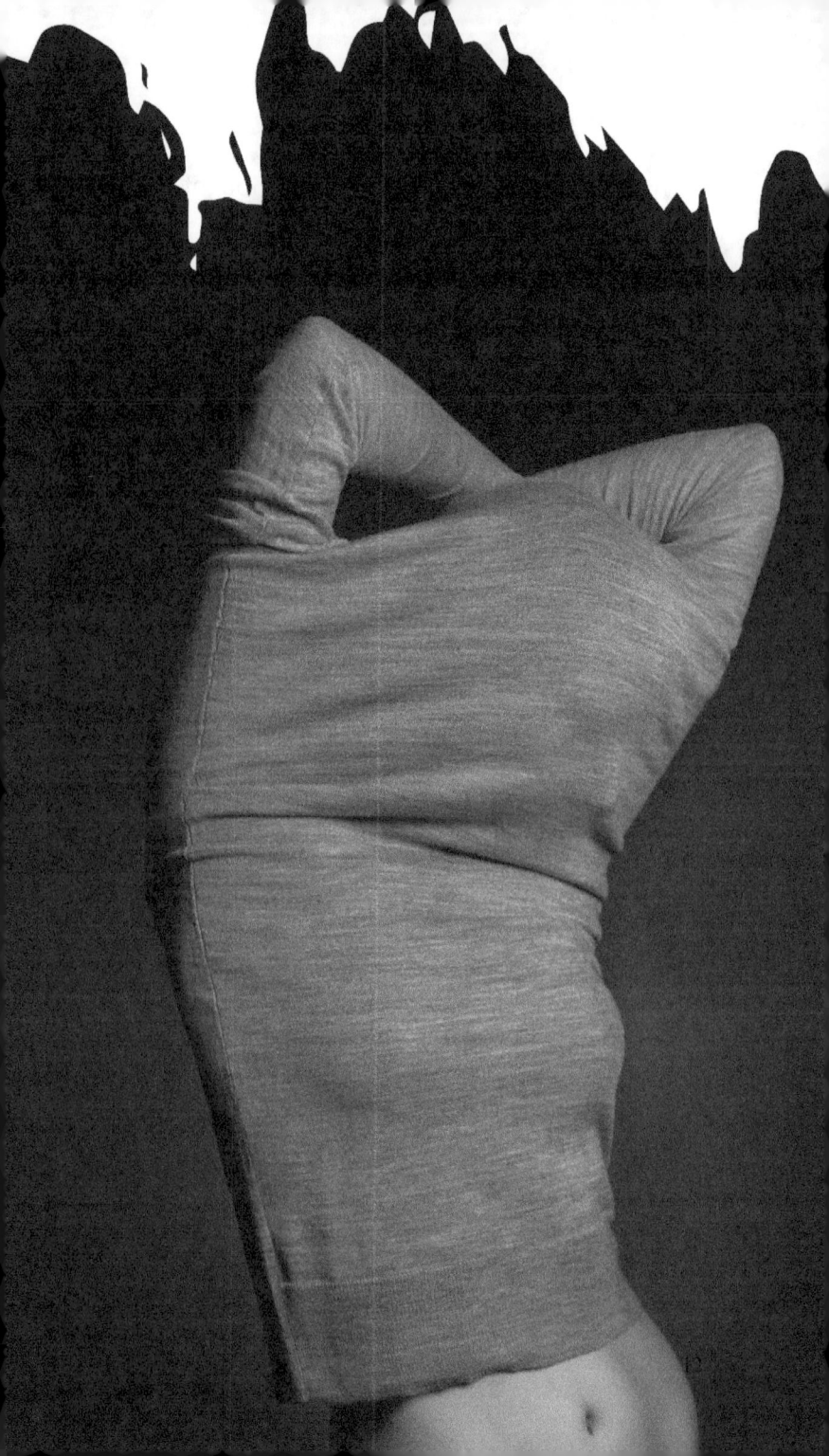

Two

Three days. That was how long I had spent in my home before I decided it was okay to go back out into the world again. Seeing those children in the park had saddened me so much that I had spent the last seventy-two hours holed up indoors, with the blinds closed, watching chick flicks, and crying into a bowl of ice cream.

I was feeling better today, definitely a lot more like myself, and wanted to try this being an adult thing again. I wasn't exactly sure where I was going today, but once I had pulled on my black, denim shorts, loose hunter-green t-shirt, and pulled my long, wavy black hair back into a ponytail, I wanted out. It was the first time I had actually gotten out of my pajamas in the past few days, and I wanted some fresh air.

My black flip-flops slapped along the pavement as soon as I walked out of my house and down the driveway. I walked past my white, Maserati Ghibli without a glance, and took to the sidewalk like a woman on a mission.

It was a beautiful spring day in Stuart, Florida, and I figured I would walk the couple of miles it was to the beach. I always liked it there because the water was so clean and the waves that lolled lazily against the shore were welcoming. A day in the cancerous sun with my feet in the golden sand would probably be enough for me to stay happy for twenty four hours.

Stuart was small and private, which is why I had relocated here. The population was about thirteen thousand, and the chances that I would run into someone from my past were slim to none. I thought it would be the perfect place for a fresh start, even after eight years.

None of the shadows looked like Mr. Spears, and my nightmares didn't include my parents anymore. I looked at that as an accomplishment; even though it took three years.

I finally made it to the beach, and sat down in my usual spot a few feet away from the empty lifeguard post. As I looked out over the ocean, I thought about how I liked this part of the beach the best because there was never anyone in the chair. Since it looked like it would fall over at any moment, the other beachgoers would stay far away from it.

I didn't mind it. Hell, I was hoping that one day it *would* fall over and possibly take me out. It would be a small mercy to keep my demons away, and the best thing for anyone who knew me.

Part of the reason I ran so far away from home was because I didn't want to damage anyone else. I decided to let myself drown in the darkness that had built up inside of me since my baby was taken from me; to let the sadness and pain consume me... so it wouldn't hurt anyone else.

Of course, I hadn't exactly left on good terms. I sat my parents down, and told them how much I hated them for abandoning me when I needed them the most. I told them that I wished they would die slow, painful deaths, and never think of me again. I sure as hell didn't plan to think of them.

Their faces were a mixture of shock, hurt, and maybe even a dash of relief. It was something that I let the demons inside of me hold closely. I wanted them to drown in my sorrow and hatred for them, and leaving was the only way I knew how to make it happen.

To me, that was the only truly beautiful thing left in this filthy world. Knowing on the inside, I had killed them over and over, with each death more horrible than the last.

But that was just a passing thought these days. I had been making progress and moving on from that moment, even though it would always creep up on me whenever I acknowledged my scar. I liked to think that though I was as damaged as I was, maybe I did have hope.

I pushed the stray hair from my face that the breeze had shaken loose and sighed. I wouldn't dwell on those thoughts right now. This was my calm moment, right before the proverbial storm that always hit, and I was going to enjoy it.

I pulled off my t-shirt so I could lay it out behind me, and laid down on top of it, crossing my arms behind my head. I didn't care that I was lying there in my bra. My scar was hidden because I was lucky enough to have the crescent shape hidden well; having been cut open above the pelvic bone.

I took a deep breath and let it out, repeating the act three times until I felt myself go to my comfortable place. I never thought of it as a 'happy place', because I was certain I didn't have one.

It took me almost no time to fall asleep. Something that would take hours of tossing and turning in my bed, was done easily enough on the sand with the ocean nearby. I'd been meaning to buy a sound machine, but I always forgot.

It wasn't long before I was startled awake. A beach ball had landed near me, spraying sand all over me and I sat up to see who the culprit was. A pair of teenage boys with sheepish looks on their faces ran over to me.

"Sorry! I told him not to hit it so hard," the one with the bright red swim shorts said.

"It's okay," I replied with a smile. I retrieved the ball from the other side of me and handed it to him, waving as they ran off.

I started to lie back down, but a sudden, bad feeling in the pit of my stomach kept me from going back to the world of dreamless sleep. I sat up and looked around, wondering if it was maybe someone watching me. After the boys had disappeared from view, there was no one near me. Upon further inspection, I noticed there was barely anyone left on the beach.

So, why do I have such a bad feeling all of a sudden?

I got to my feet and grabbed my shirt, shaking loose any sand that had managed to stick to it, before I pulled it over my head. I put my hands on my hips for a moment, and took one last sweeping look around the area until I was satisfied that I wasn't being watched.

I ran back home with my flip-flops in my hand, trying to figure out what had suddenly shaken me so badly.

Three

After I'd showered and dried my hair, I went into my bedroom and sat down at my desk. I adjusted my towel to keep it firmly wrapped around my body, and flipped open my laptop. I decided to surf the internet and see if anything major had happened in the news. Realizing nothing of note was there, I decided to go to the *Los Angeles Times* obituaries and began my regular routine of searching for my parents' names.

I spent a good fifteen minutes scrolling through all of the names. I liked to take my time and go slowly—a personal form of torture—and was just about to close my laptop when I saw it.

A name I recognized. A name belonging to someone I loved. A name that wasn't Mom *or* Dad.

"Frances Robert Lettsworth, aged 84, entered into eternal rest on Friday..."

I stared at the picture next to the headline and felt tears start to sting my eyes. All of the sadness I had been feeling was suddenly making sense. Even though I didn't know my grandfather had died until just now, I understood I was feeling things that bothered me more than usual. For as long as I could remember, I had an amazing relationship with that man. I kept in touch with him during the first few years I was gone, but after a while, each time I tried to reach out there would be no answer. I wasn't sure why, but now...

This was the second time in my life that I had ever experienced what I would consider true heartbreak. The feeling of someone punching a hole into my chest while wearing a pair of spiked, brass knuckles–puncturing my life source–was the only way to explain it. The slow bleeding out, the ragged hole in my heart; it was happening again and I wasn't sure if I could deal with it this time.

I couldn't bring myself to read the rest of the obituary. My wanting and waiting for my parents to die had backfired on me. Grandpa Frances was my mother's father, and she was the one who'd shut me out before my father did. I remember the phone calls with Grandpa like they happened yesterday. He would tell me how angry he was with her for what she did to me, that he loved me very much, and how I always had a home with him and Grandma.

I closed my eyes for a moment and let the tears escape. He was worth the tears, the sorrow, and the heartache. I would let myself cry for him, and while I allowed myself to grieve, I opened another tab on Chrome and pulled up travel websites. I wouldn't let my mother or father keep me away from the funeral. They could fight me when I got there, they could curse my name and the day I was born, but I was going to see Grandpa Frances one last time, and there wasn't a damn thing they could do to stop me.

I skimmed the announcement to see when the services would be held, and realized that I would have to leave tomorrow. His funeral was going to be held on Tuesday, followed by the burial on Wednesday–and today was Sunday.

With a deep breath, I went back to the travel page and booked my flight. It cost a hell of a lot more than it should have, but, it was a last minute thing and afterward, per their company policy, I would be able to get some money back for bereavement..

Once the reservations, including hotel and car, were taken care of, I shut down my laptop. I stood up and pulled my towel off, making sure I was dry, before I went over to my bed and got dressed in the clothes I had laid out. I decided that today was going to be another bowl of ice cream and chick-flick day, so the bra wasn't necessary. I reached for my loose, gray sweatpants and pulled them on, followed by a black, ribbed tank top, and sighed.

Some days are just meant for tears and ice cream, I thought miserably as I left my room and went to the kitchen.

Four

At 3am the next morning, I was in my car and heading to Orlando International Airport. There were closer airports to fly out of, but I always liked that one because it was bigger, and I knew the layout. It took me just under two hours to get there, and I let the valet take my car. I gave him a larger tip than he was used to, and told him to take good care of my car.

Money was never a concern to me. Grandpa Frances had put some money into a high yield trust for me when I was born, and every now and then I would go in and take some out. Twenty-eight years of interest meant I would be able to live a very comfortable life, and I knew that as long as I left something in there, the interest accrued would continue to pay back more than what I took out.

I was mindful of what I spent, even though I knew I didn't have to be. The most expensive things I had purchased with cash were my home and car, because I didn't want to have to deal with remembering when the payments were due. Not to mention, doing it that way meant that I finally had something that belonged to *me,* and no one could take it away.

With my carry-on bag over my shoulder, I walked through the main doors and looked at the information board for American Airlines departures. Once I found the gate I would be leaving from, I made my way to security and waited. The line wasn't as long as I expected it to be, but I always liked to arrive early so I didn't get stuck in line, with the potential of missing my flight. I put my bag down and let out my breath in a huff as the people in front of me trudged slowly along. When I finally reached the front of the line, I picked up the bag I had been kicking along, and pulled my ID out.

The TSA agent scrutinized my ID for a good three minutes before he was satisfied that I was, indeed, the smiling Zaydee G. Lansing in the photo, and handed it back to me. I understood, though. I hadn't smiled in such a long time, and I walked around with such a stoic look on my face, that when I had to show my ID for any reason, everyone usually did a double take.

"Thanks," I mumbled as I took my ID and put it back into my bag.

I quickly found my gate and sat down in the section of half empty chairs, choosing one that would face the window, so I could watch the sun as it started to break over the horizon. An hour later, the flight attendant started to call rows. I never did get to see the sun come up because when she called first class, I stood up and grabbed my bag. I walked over to the small podium, handed the ticket to the woman in the red and blue uniform, and waited until she nodded for me to continue to the plane.

There were only three of us in first class, so it took no time to pop my carry-on overhead and get comfortable while I waited for everyone else to board. The only reason I ever liked to fly first class was because it was first on and first off. I hated waiting in lines–patience never being a virtue I possessed–and instead of being in a shitty mood when I reached my destinations, I always bought first class when I traveled.

I rested my head against the back of the chair and closed my eyes, securing my seat belt blindly. I couldn't recall a time that I had ever comfortably slept on an airplane, but I was going to give it one hell of a try. I was going to have a hard couple of weeks in front of me, and I needed to arrive fresh and ready to take on whatever hell my family would be throwing at me.

My head rolled slightly to the right, and as the plane started to take off, I slipped away into another dreamless sleep. What felt like minutes later, I felt a hand gently rocking my shoulder and I opened my eyes groggily. I glanced out the window and smiled slightly at the sight of the LAX runway.

"Thanks," I said to the flight attendant in a thick voice, stretching my arms over my head. She smiled at me and nodded before she moved on. I assumed she was looking for more potential sleepers, but I didn't stick around long enough to find out. I retrieved my bag and headed out of the plane and down the runway toward the airport baggage claim area.

I stood as close to the conveyor belt as I could, and waited until I saw the blue piece of silk I always tied to my bags. It made them easier to pick out and it would also mean less time spent standing among people I didn't know. Once I had my bags, I went down to the lower level and walked over to the rental car counters. I found the company I had my reservation with and went through whatever process they needed from me so I could get the keys as quickly as possible and leave.

Once everything was signed and the keys were handed to me, I gave a quick, tight smile to the representative and walked out of the airport toward the parking garage across the street. According to what I had just been told, the rental cars were on the fifth floor, and mine would be in the third row in a spot marked 24. When I got to the sleek, black Cadillac Escalade, I popped open the trunk and threw my bags in.

After I closed it, I turned around and slumped against the back of the SUV. Every fiber inside of me was telling me to just go back to the car rental counter, hand them their keys, and take the next flight back to Orlando, but I knew I couldn't. I had come this far, and the very least I could do was pay my final respects to the greatest man I had ever known.

Five

I had spent what was left of my Monday picking out something respectable to wear. I had brought almost every dress, skirt, and blouse I owned. I finally settled on a pretty, brand-new, black halter dress with a wide, white stripe around the waist. I paired it off with a white shrug and slipped on my best shoes; a pair of white Nine West dress slip-ons.

I left the hotel room on Tuesday morning at eleven-thirty-five, and drove the ten miles to the funeral home. When I pulled into the parking lot, I saw that it was almost full and smiled, thinking of how many other people loved Grandpa Frances besides me. I saw an open spot near the back of the parking lot, and backed in.

Cutting the engine, I rested an elbow on the window and pressed my hand against my forehead. I had suddenly developed a huge headache, no doubt from knowing what was waiting for me once I went through those doors. I desperately wanted to see Grandpa again, but not like this.

It's too late to back out now, Zee. Get out of the car and get it over with.

I entered the funeral home timidly. I hadn't seen my parents—or any of my family for that matter—in ten years, and I wasn't sure if I would be welcome. I loved my grandfather dearly, though, and if anyone tried to keep me from paying my respects; I would leave quietly and just show up at the burial. Out of respect to him I wouldn't cause a scene, but they wouldn't be able to ban me from public property.

With a shaky hand, I pulled open the black, iron door handle and walked into the dimly lit hallway full of people. I kept my head down as I walked over to the open book and signed my name, taking a prayer card and dropping it into my purse. Out of the corner of my eye, I could see the casket and the top of my grandfather's head. I didn't want to go in just yet though, because the wailing coming from who I assumed to be my mother made me nervous.

How was she going to react to my being here? Would she hug me and tell me she missed me? Or would she get angry and yell at me to leave?

I bit my lip and decided to go over to the board with pictures on it. It would buy me some time, and I would at least have something to hold my attention for a while. I quietly made my way past the groups of people that were standing in various locations in the room until I made it to the picture board.

The first photo in the top left corner made me smile. It was a picture of Grandpa in his early twenties, looking dapper as ever in a suit and tie, with a cigarette in his hand. I wasn't sure what exactly had happened on that day that had warranted such fancy clothes, but he was laughing in the picture. Even though it was black and white, I could still see the sparkle in his brilliant blue eyes. His dark-blonde hair was slicked back and every hair was neatly kept in place. Grandpa had been like that his entire life though; very proud of his appearance and always making sure he looked neat.

My eyes wandered from picture to picture. The one of him and Mom when she was about five years old, looking up at him with adoring eyes and a smile so wide that you could see she was missing her front teeth. I looked at each picture in turn, a sad smile etched across my lips until I finally reached the end. The feeling of sadness gave way to anger when I saw that one of the pictures that should have been me and my grandfather had been ripped down the middle so it was just him.

I knew I should've stayed away from this.

A hand on my shoulder brought my attention away from the picture board of now broken pictures and torn memories. Shrugging the hand off, I turned around to address whoever it was and came face to face with the tired eyes of my father.

"I thought that was you, Zaydee," he said quietly. I crossed my arms firmly over my chest as he slid his hands into his pants pockets and sighed. "How did you find out about this?"

"I check the online obits from time to time to see if any of you are dead. Unfortunately, it turned out to be Grandpa," I replied in a snarky tone.

For a moment his face darkened, but he seemed to relent on his feeling of whatever had come over him, because he knew I had a point. It was a miracle in itself that I was even standing there having a conversation with him, so he knew not to push me too far.

"Are you going to go in?" he finally asked, running a hand over his face.

"I'd like to, but I don't know how she'll react to me being here," I admitted, jutting my chin toward the room full of mourners.

"She's so wrapped up in her grief right

now; I'm not sure she thinks anyone else is here with her. Come on, I'll walk you in," he said, holding out an arm.

I didn't uncross my arms and I didn't move from my spot. I didn't understand why he was holding out his arm to me, because I and my parents had parted on such bad terms, that I had every right to break it in five places if I wanted to. I let my eyes travel from his outstretched arm to his face to see if there was any sign of deception, but I couldn't find any, so I relented and took his arm with a grunt.

"It's good to have you home, Sweetheart," he said quietly and patted the top of my hand.

I rolled my eyes as he walked me into the room and straight up to my grandfather's polished, maple casket with beautiful white lining.

"Take as much time as you need," he said gently, as I let go of his arm and put my hands on the edge of the beautiful box that held only death on the inside. It was a reminder of yet another masquerade of beauty that was shattered by the realism of what it had been truly made for.

"Hi, Grandpa," I said softly, reaching up to stroke his white hair. "I missed you. I'm sorry it took me too long to come see you. I hope you know that I've always loved you and always will. I'll see you soon."

The tears that started to fall probably made me look weaker than I felt. They weren't solely tears of sorrow, they were tears of anger. I could have had the chance to be with him in his final moments, but because of Mom, Dad, and Mr. Spears, I ran as far as I could when the moment presented itself. Because of them I refused to come back and even see Grandpa, telling him that I would always try my best then pushing it to the back of my mind. And now it was too late. I'd never hear his gentle voice, or feel his soft, strong arms around me again. All I had with him was this moment; where he was lying in a casket void of life and looking more peaceful than I could remember.

I felt Dad's hand on my shoulder again

and I quickly wiped the tears away from my face.

"He always loved you so much, Zaydee," he said quietly.

"I know."

I turned to nod at Dad before I walked away from the casket and settled into the very back row of the room. He looked at me with sad eyes and shook his head as he sat down next to Mom and the priest entered the room. I was sitting next to some people I didn't know, but it was as far away from my family as I could get, so I decided to take it and just wait for the services to be over then go back to my hotel room. I'd probably spend the whole of the two weeks shut in there as a defense mechanism against the sadness, but I really didn't want to. I had another reason for coming back; not nearly as important as Grandpa, but there were questions that I needed answered.

As the priest took his place at the podium, I took a deep breath and let out a gut wrenching sob.

I'm so sorry, Grandpa.

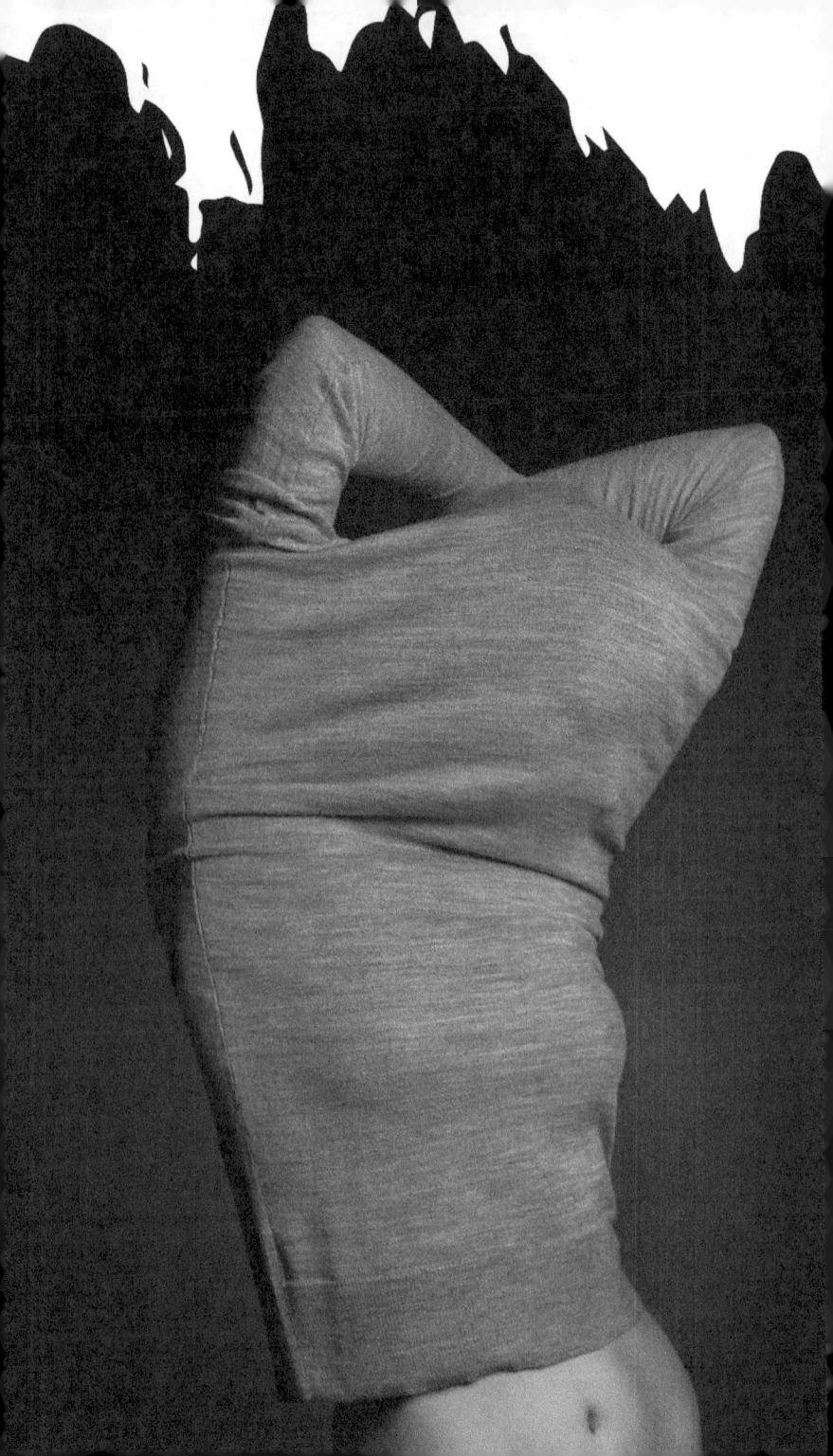

Six

After the services were over, my father stopped me as I was walking out the back door. He told me he would really like it if I came over for dinner that night and that Mom would too. It had taken everything inside of me not to roll my eyes, but I accepted because I really didn't feel like going out to a restaurant, and I didn't know if the hotel food was any good.

I did go back and change my clothes though. I didn't want to go back to a place of broken memories in my funeral attire, no matter how appropriate it would have been. I chose a light blue sundress and a pair of white flip-flops for the occasion. I remember reading somewhere that blue was the color for stability and confidence, and that was exactly what I needed to be able to survive dinner with them.

Around 4pm that afternoon, I left the hotel. Dinner was going to be around six, but Dad had asked me to come over early so we could catch up. My knuckles were white because of how tightly I was gripping the steering wheel, and I kept fighting down the waves of nausea that were threatening to make me sick.

This evening was definitely going to show me if I had any of that fourteen year old bravery left inside of me.

I pulled up in front of their house twenty minutes later and hopped out of the SUV. I took a deep breath, adjusted my purse on my shoulder, and walked up to the door. My finger hovered over the doorbell button for a moment. *Did I really want to do this?* I hadn't come all this way for them, and I really didn't know what good would come out of this anyway.

The choice was taken out of my hands when the front door flew open. I jumped and pulled my hand away from the doorbell, and

Dad smiled sheepishly.

"I saw you coming up the walkway," he admitted.

"Oh."

"Come in, Zaydee," he said, stepping back and motioning with his arm.

I nodded and walked through the open door. I crossed my arms over my chest and glanced around, realizing that not much had changed since I had left. The family pictures were still hanging on the wall in the living room; which surprised me, and they seemed to have the same old couches they bought when I was a kid.

Maybe I'll send them some new stuff. Depending on how this goes, anyway.

"So, how have you been?" he asked, as he led the way into the living room and sat down. I decided to sit in the old rocking chair in the corner of the room and shrugged.

"Rita! Zaydee is here," he suddenly called out.

I cringed. I didn't expect to have to see her so quickly after walking through the door, but this was their home and I couldn't exactly forbid her from coming into her own living room.

In she walked, a carefully blank look on her face as she went over and sat next to my father. The silence that followed her entrance was deafening. Dad awkwardly put an arm around my mother, and I looked down at my fingernails. When I started to pick the skin around them, Mom spoke up.

"Don't do that; you know how much I hate it when you do that," she said quietly.

I sighed loudly and dropped my hands onto my lap. Mom looked away, Dad looked sad, and I just looked annoyed. I didn't come for a "you're in my house, you'll obey my rules" dinner. Truth be told, the only reason I came was for the free food and maybe a quick look around.

"Sorry," she muttered.

I didn't respond. I didn't even look at

her anymore, instead I turned my attention to my father and gave him a tight smile. I guess it would be as good a time as any to ask him something that had been weighing on my mind since I left the wake earlier.

I wasn't sure how to word it, or how to even bring it up, but the curiosity in me was piquing at an all-time high and I needed to know.

"Hey Dad?" I asked timidly.

"Yes honey?"

"Does Mr. Spears still teach over at Rockford High?"

"No. He hasn't been a teacher in about, oh, I'd say five years. Does that sound about right, Rita? Yeah, five years. Why do you ask?"

"I was just thinking of going to see him," I replied quietly.

"He always was your favorite teacher," he said warmly. "You'll be happy to know that three years after you left, he actually got promoted to principal. He's still at Rockford, just not as a teacher."

Let's see. If I'm twenty-eight and he was thirty-eight at the time, he would be ... Fifty-two? Yeah. Fifty-two.

"I'm sure he'd be quite happy to see you, Zay. He loves seeing his old students," Dad said pleasantly.

"Hm," I mumbled.

I was curious as to what he would look like. He had been so damn handsome when I'd looked at him through childish eyes, so it made me wonder if he would look the same to me through adult eyes. Did he still have the same dark brown hair, or had it grayed some? Were his kind brown eyes as warm as ever, or had they grown as cold as they were after I had given birth? I didn't know, but I decided that tomorrow, after the burial, I would go find out. I didn't have anything to lose or gain from it, and I was honestly curious to see if he would speak to me.

Seven

As I drove back to my hotel, I thought of how uneventful dinner was. I felt like I had been eating in a monastery, surrounded by monks who had taken a vow of silence. The only sounds in the dining room were the occasional throat clearing, the sipping of wine, silver-wear on the plates, and my mumbled "thank you" when it was over.

I sighed when I reached the red light a few blocks away, and put a hand against my forehead. Of the two, Dad seemed to be the one that genuinely liked having me in the house. Mom, I kind of understood. We had just gotten back from viewing her father in a casket, so I didn't expect a parade of glitter and rainbows.

I glanced at the time on the

dashboard. It was six-thirty-one, which meant I had gotten out of there faster than I thought I would. I was happy about that. I didn't want to sit in that house any longer than I had to, making small talk with the two people who had damaged me the most.

An angry car honk behind me shook me from my thoughts. I put my foot gently on the gas and took a left turn, catching every green light on the way back. Once I parked, I had an idea. It was a slim to no chance, but I thought I would give it a try anyway.

I walked through the lobby doors and went up to the counter, drumming my fingers along the wooden top while waiting for someone to notice me.

"Good evening! How can I help you?" the young girl with the bright, bleached smile asked.

"I need a phone book please," I replied quietly.

"Sure thing!" she said as she bounced away from the counter. I glanced up at the huge, flatscreen television that sat on the wall behind where she had been standing and watched the news. A few minutes later, she came back, her smile wide as ever as she handed it over to me.

"Thanks."

I held the phone book tightly against my chest as I walked down the hallway toward the elevators. I punched the button to call one of them down and waited. A moment later, I heard a ding as the doors to the elevator across from me opened. I entered, glanced at the numbers and pushed number five. Then I leaned back against the elevator wall, waiting while it slowly climbed to my designated floor.

I waited impatiently for the slow doors to open before I walked out and turned right. My room was all the way at the end of the hall and was the largest one on the floor, because I had requested it.

I fished around in my purse until I found the room card and slid it in quickly. The door unlocked quietly and I cast a glance down the hallway before I walked in, locking it firmly behind me.

With a sigh, I dropped my purse by the door and went over to the lush, king-sized bed that sat against the wall in the middle of the room and sat down. I bit my lip and wondered if what I was about to do was a good idea, if the information presented itself, but I decided I didn't care and opened the book, flipping until I found the administration phone number for the school.

Here goes nothing, I thought as I leaned back and grabbed the phone from where it sat on the bedside table and began to punch in the numbers. My hands were shaking, so I wrapped one around the phone cord, waiting as the phone rang once, twice, three times.

I had given up and was halfway to hanging up the phone when someone picked up.

"Rockford High, this is Principal Spears," the deep voice said.

I panicked. I hadn't expected him to be the one to answer. Hell, I hadn't expected anyone to still be there at all since it was damn near seven at night.

"Hey, stranger," I chirped.

"Who is this?" he demanded, the sound of papers rustling in the background.

"Oh yeah. Ha-ha," I replied nervously with a choked giggle. "It's um, Zaydee Lansing."

The papers immediately stopped rustling as Mr. Spears tried to process the information. I felt like years passed before he finally spoke again, and in that time, I'd convinced myself over and over not to hang up on him. He already knew who I was, so it wouldn't serve anything to disconnect the call before I had my answers.

"It's been a long time, Zaydee," he said, quietly.

"Yeah. So, principal, huh? Congratulations," I said. My voice was shaking and I had to clear my throat a few times to get a better grip on myself.

"Thank you. To what do I owe the pleasure?" he asked curiously.

"Um, I'm back in town. My grandfather died, so you know, I had to make an appearance," I replied.

Stop sounding like an imbecile, I scolded myself.

"And I was wondering if you'd be interested in lunch tomorrow?"

He stayed quiet. Probably trying to decipher my intentions for getting together, but truth be told, I knew no matter how much I wanted to, I'd never be able to ask him what I wanted to know over the phone.

"Why don't you just come over to the school? I'll be here for another few hours getting some paperwork straightened out," he finally said.

"Sure, I guess. Give me a little bit to change and I'll be right over," I replied.

"See you soon, then," he said kindly.

"Okay."

Neither of us hung up right away. We both sat there listening to the other one breathing until he finally relented and disconnected the call.

I got up from the bed and sat right back down. I didn't realize I was so unsteady after what I had just done until I tried to get to my feet. *Why was I doing this?* He was the only man who had ever broken my heart, and I was wanting nothing more than to sit down with him.

I gave myself at least ten minutes before I got up again and went to my bags. I pulled out a pair of fitted, yellow denim shorts and a white fitted V-neck shirt. I was pretty sure I had brought my yellow flip-flops with me, and that would make the outfit. I rummaged around the bag for a fresh pair of panties and bra before I headed to the bathroom to take a shower.

As I turned on the water and undressed myself, I caught a glimpse of my face in the mirror and sighed. I didn't even realize I had been smiling. No matter how bad this was going to be for me, it still apparently made me happy that Mr. Spears had agreed to meet with me.

I shook my head as I undressed and stepped into the stream of hot water.

Better late than never.

Eight

The security post at the gates of the high school was empty so I drove right by it. I parked in the student section of the parking lot, and gave myself one last glance in the rear-view mirror before I hopped out and headed toward the main entrance. I wasn't sure how I was going to get in, because the school had been closed for hours, but the closer I got, the more nervous I became.

"I almost went back to my office," he said, pushing one of the double doors open for me.

He hadn't changed much, with the exception of a few extra lines on his face, and his hair having a few gray patches here and there. He was still the same man I remembered from my teenage years;

ruggedly handsome, tall, and slightly built.

"Sorry. I had some stuff to do first," I mumbled, looking at my feet.

"It's good to see you again, Zaydee," he said, reaching forward and giving me an awkward hug.

I patted his back a couple of times before I pulled away and glanced up at him. His eyes had that warm smile I ended up missing during the rest of my years at Rockford High. Maybe he wasn't angry with me anymore, maybe he was just trying to be nice. I would find out soon enough.

"Come on in," he said, stepping back. I walked just inside the doors and waited for him to lock up again, before he motioned for me to follow him down the hallway.

Mr. Spears led the way past the secretary's desk and into his office, and sat down in his big leather chair. He smoothed out his black and white striped tie, and rolled up the sleeves of his crisp white dress shirt before crossing his hands on the large, polished oak table.

"I'm sorry for your loss," he said, giving me a sympathetic look. "Which grandfather was it, if you don't mind me asking?"

"Frances," I replied. "My mother's dad."

"Frances?" he asked with a shocked look on his face. "I wish I had known that. I would have gone to the services today."

I raised a curious eyebrow. Why would he want to attend my grandfather's wake?

A pleasant smile crossed his face. "Frances was a great man, Zaydee. He and I became close after you left."

I nodded and crossed my arms over my chest, slumping a little in my seat. I wasn't going to ask any more questions on the subject. I didn't want to know why they had become so close, I just wanted to know certain things and now was my chance.

"Mr. Spears—"

"Garret," he said, waving his hand,

"You're not my student anymore."

My eyes fell on his left hand when he put it back down. There used to be a bright, golden wedding band on his ring finger when I lived here, and now it was gone.

"What happened there?" I asked, keeping my eyes on his hand.

"Huh? Oh. I told her. I waited for the statute of limitations to run out and I told her. Not because I felt what we did was wrong, but because I knew she would be vindictive enough to turn me in for loving someone else. I didn't exactly tell her all of it, but enough for her to leave," he replied with a shrug, leaning back in his chair.

"I'm sorry," I said quietly.

"Nothing to be sorry about, Zaydee. It was as much my fault, maybe even more so than yours. But I'm sure that's not why you're here. Or is it?"

I shook my head truthfully. It really wasn't why I was there, sitting in the principal's office, across from my biggest mistake and greatest heartbreak.

"Then what's on your mind, kiddo?" he asked curiously.

I rolled my eyes, but caught myself when he started to laugh. It was obvious that his "kiddo" remark struck a nerve in me.

"Well, I uh ..." I swallowed the lump that was forming in my throat. I didn't know how to ask what I wanted to ask without cutting open an old scar. The one thing I learned about scars was that they never healed if you kept reopening them.

"It was a boy," he said softly.

I looked up from my lap and looked into his eyes. I felt tears immediately start spilling over, and I had to bite my lip to keep from letting out a sob.

Garrett took a box of Kleenex out of one of his top drawers and set it in the middle of his desk. I reached forward and grabbed a tissue, dabbing at my eyes.

"His name is Scott, and this," he said,

pulling open the top drawer again and producing a four by six photograph, "is the only picture I have of him. He was eight in this."

I reached for the picture and held it up so that I could see the little boy smiling on a bicycle. That was all it took for me to burst into gut-wrenching sobs. I never expected that I would ever get to know what I had, let alone see his face at one point in his life.

Garrett sighed and got to his feet. I heard the wheels in his chair rolling as he pushed his chair back and came over to put an arm around me.

I rested my head against his shoulder and cried as I held up the picture of Scott and looked at him. I was thankful that someone loved him enough to make him smile, and I was even more thankful that he had been taken from me. There was no way in hell that I would have ever made him as happy as he was in that picture.

"Frances always had my gratitude for what he did," Garrett said softly, as he ran his hand up and down my arm in an effort to calm me.

I pulled away from him and took a deep, shuddering breath. I didn't know what he was talking about but I couldn't form the words to ask him either.

"Didn't you know?" he asked, moving to sit at the edge of his desk. "Frances and Greta adopted Scott. They sent him to live with your aunt and uncle in Phoenix because they knew they couldn't raise him."

"What?" I blurted out. My voice was a mixture of rage and sorrow. How was it possible that my parents had kept this from me? They let me suffer for the last four years I lived with them without telling me?

Garrett ran a hand over his face before crossing his arms. "Frances and I became close after it happened. He came to school one day and asked me if I was the father. I don't know how he knew it, maybe all of those times I kept you after school, but I didn't lie to him. I knew he was an honorable enough man that he would keep the secret. I confessed to him and begged him to forgive me, and he did. He told me that he and Greta had already set up the adoption but not to tell you, because he didn't want you to chase after Scott at such a young age. He wanted you to get your education and eventually they would tell you. That's why I was such a bastard toward you, Zaydee. I had to be. I didn't know any other way to keep my part of the deal with Frances if we continued on with whatever it was we had."

I took another steadying breath and used the back of my hands to wipe the remaining tears from my face. I was angry now. Angry that my entire family had kept this secret from me. Angry that Garrett probably had spent time with Scott and I hadn't. Angry that they didn't think I was worthy enough to know something as important as this.

"I have to go," I announced as I promptly got to my feet.

"Zaydee, wait," Garrett said, grabbing me by my arm. "If you're anything like I remember, your temper is going to make you do something you'll regret later."

I pulled my arm away from him violently.

"Get over yourself, *Garrett*. You don't know me. You were the first one who tucked tail and ran when I needed someone the most," I spat at him.

"That's not fair. I told you why—"

I cut him off as I turned on my heel and headed for the office door. He had just given me enough information to find my son, and nothing was going to stop me from going to see him.

"Zaydee Lansing, I'm speaking to you," he boomed as he reached over my head and pushed the door closed.

"Get out of the way! You have no right to keep me here!" I screamed, turning to swat at him.

He moved quickly and caught my arms by the wrists, then held them over my head against the door. Garrett always was strong, but his height added to his strength, and then there was me, barely scraping over five feet and I was no match for him.

"I'm not letting you leave until you promise me that you're not going to do anything stupid," he said sternly.

"I already have one father, I don't need a second one," I replied through gritted teeth as I struggled to free myself from his grip.

"Stop trying to get away from me," he said in a thick voice.

I angrily tried to shove my body against him in an attempt to shake him loose, but it didn't work. It didn't have the reaction I was expecting. Instead of making him let go, he pressed himself against me and crushed his lips passionately against mine.

I allowed the moment. I hadn't been with a man since Garrett because I didn't want to feel the pain of heartbreak again, but this wasn't why I wanted to see him. It wasn't why I needed to sit across from him and talk to him, but his kiss was so hungry that I allowed it.

When he pulled away from me, his breaths heavy with passion and lust, I gave my wrists a gentle tug. He smiled sadly and finally let me go.

It was my moment to leave; to walk out the door and I took it. I couldn't stand there and kiss him, feeling what I felt for him come back to me and stay, without trying anything more.

And I just wasn't ready for that yet.

Nine

When I woke up the next morning, I quickly put on a black strapless dress and black shrug. I found my black flip-flops and put them back on, because after I looked at the clock, I realized if I tried to stop to find a nice pair of dress shoes, I'd be late to Grandpa Frances' burial.

I ran down the hallway and decided to take the stairs. I didn't want to lose any more time waiting for the elevator, and by the time I got into my rental, I realized I'd probably have to drive straight to the cemetery. I reached for my purse that I had tossed into the passenger seat, and pulled out the information I had gotten from the viewing, then set the location for Saint Raphael's Cemetery into my GPS before I took off.

I drove aggressively all the way to the cemetery grounds. I cursed loudly at people who lingered at the green lights, and drove around people I felt were driving too slow.

Once I got to the wide iron gates, I slowed down and drove the recommended five mile-per-hour speed limit. After all, what the GPS said should have taken me twenty five minutes, only ended up taking fifteen due to speeding.

The curves and bends in the cemetery lead me around in all directions. To the back, to the front, to either side, and had me to the point of such frustration that I was considering going back to the office and asking where to go, when I saw the only excavator on the property sitting in the far right back corner. I turned the truck around the bend and made my way over just in time for the funeral procession to start coming my way.

Jesus Christ. This shouldn't have been so difficult, I thought angrily.

I waited inside until the hearse

carrying my grandfather, and the cars following had stopped. I waited while the mourners got out of their cars, and only jumped out when I saw my parents. I made a beeline straight for my father.

"I want to talk to you when this is all over," I said to him quietly, to which he nodded.

We stopped and waited while the pallbearers retrieved Grandpa's casket from the hearse and carried it to the burial spot. Mom started to cry again and I started to roll my eyes when I spotted my grandmother. She was using a cane and walking slowly toward the chairs that had been set up, holding a tissue to her nose.

I left my father's side and went over to her, putting an arm around her shoulders.

"Hi, Grandma," I said softly.

She stopped walking and looked up at me. A sad smile creased her worn lips as she put an arm around me to give me a frail hug.

"It's good to see you. I'm so glad you

came. He would be happy to know you were here," she said in a shaky voice.

I nodded and blinked back tears as I kept an arm around her tiny shoulders, walking her to the chair that sat front row center.

"Thank you, Zaydee," she said shakily. I leaned down and kissed her on her cheek before going to the back row of the ceremony and crossed my hands in front of myself.

I wasn't going to sit with the family, no matter how much they may have wanted me to. This was supposed to be about my grandfather being laid to rest and if I sat near them, it would only be a matter of time before I snapped.

The priest walked to the front and stood next to the casket. He asked us all to bow our heads as he started to pray. I looked down at my hands and clasped them. I wasn't much for prayer these days, but I could manage one or two in the memory of the greatest man I had ever known.

Once he was done, he asked if anyone had anything they wanted to say; a special memory to share.

I heard someone clear their throat before the familiar voice said, "I do."

I jerked my head up and saw the priest motioning the voice toward him. It was Garrett, and he was dressed in a dark-brown suit, white dress shirt, and black tie. His shiny black shoes crushed the grass as he walked with purpose to the front of everyone gathered.

"Greta, with your permission, I think it's time I talk about this," he said softly to her. She nodded in agreement and I glanced around nervously.

I had a sickening feeling in the pit of my stomach on what he wanted to talk about. But he wouldn't do it at my grandfather's funeral, would he? He had to have more common sense than that. As soon as he opened his mouth and started speaking, I realized I couldn't have been more wrong.

"Fourteen years ago, I destroyed a life," he began with a heavy sigh. "I destroyed a life that was very near and dear to this man whom we're here to honor today, and he forgave me for it. He knew somehow, and he still managed to find it in himself to forgive my misdeeds. He, along with his wife, did something I never expected. They stepped in to make sure that the product of my mess would stay close to the family forever; that to me was the greatest gift they could have given to me. And to Zaydee," he said looking up at me.

I was absolutely mortified. Some of my family glanced at each other and began to whisper as my father stiffened in the front row.

"Because of this man, I got to know that my son was taken care of and has been raised by people who love him. I'll always be eternally grateful for that. I know I'm not family, but he's the closest thing to a non-blood relative that I have and I will miss him as much as anyone here. Thank you, Frances," he said, as he placed a hand on the casket. "Thank you for everything."

As Garrett started to walk away from the casket, Dad got to his feet and turned to watch him. I could see the rage on his rigid body; he understood now. He now knew that the person who had fathered my child was Garrett and I could tell that he was trying to control himself. Even though I was a twenty-eight year old woman now, I'm sure he still saw me as the terrified fourteen year old who had sat them down one snowy afternoon in December to confess that I was pregnant.

"You son of a bitch," Dad seethed as Garrett walked past him.

"Larry, sit down," Mom hissed through her tears.

I watched as Garrett walked away from the entire service, got into his car, and drove away. He had just sent a shockwave through the entire family, and now that his work was done, he was leaving it open for me to fill in the blank spaces.

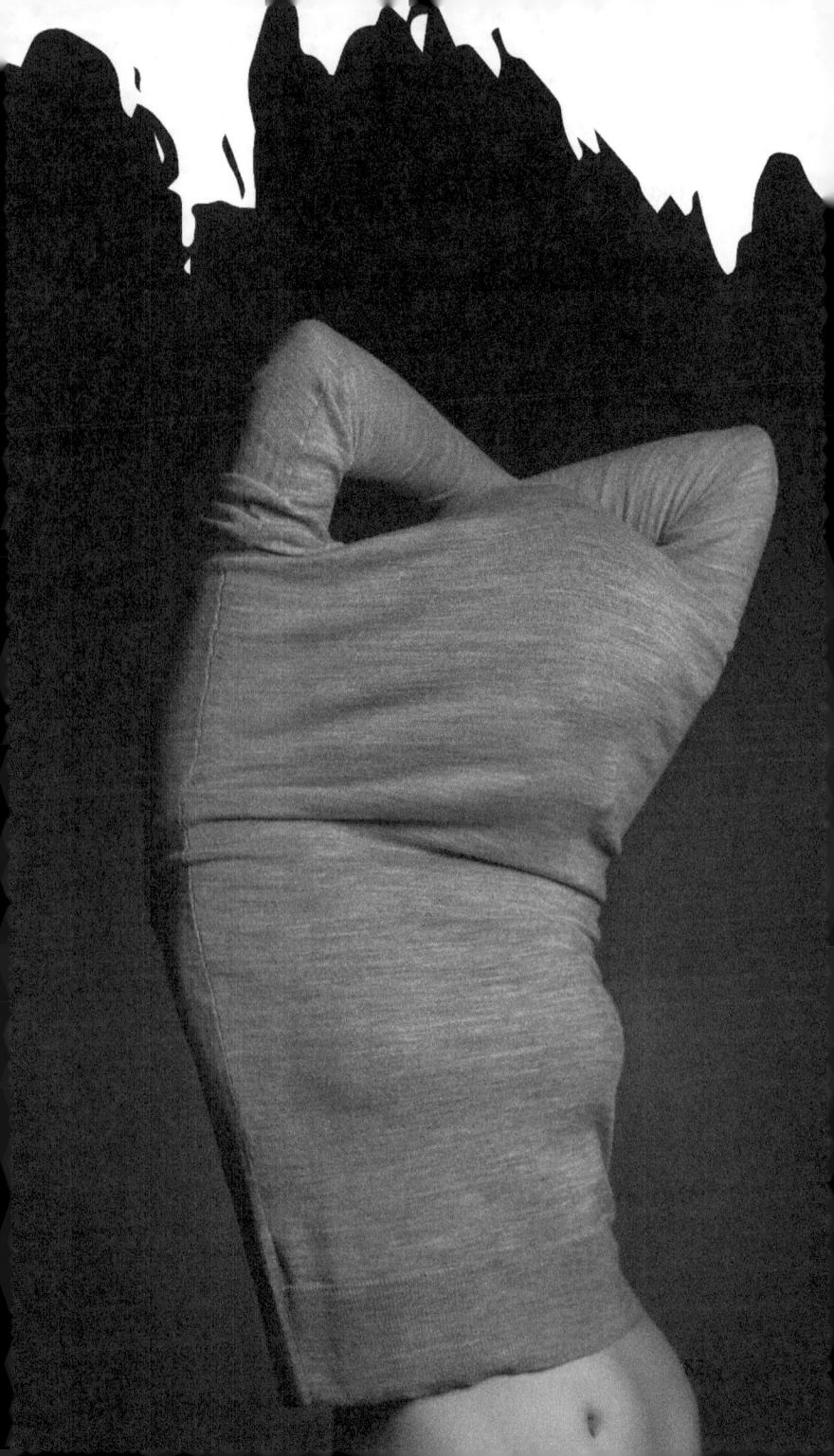

Ten

The rest of the morning was spent face-down on the bed in the hotel room. I couldn't believe that Garrett had shoved me in between a rock and a hard place and then just left.

God, the way Dad looked at me, I thought with a shudder. I grabbed the sides of the large, fluffy pillow and let out a frustrated scream. I was so angry and relieved at the same time that I didn't know what to do.

I rolled onto my back, arms and legs spread out, and stared at the ceiling. How could he have done that? Of all the times and places, at Grandpa Frances' funeral? With an angry grunt, I pushed myself up into a seated position and retrieved the phone book. I flipped the pages until I found the number for

Rockford High School again and jabbed the numbers into the phone pad. I was pissed; *really* pissed and I wasn't going to let this go.

"Rockford High School, this is Belle speaking. How may I help you?" the voice asked cheerfully.

"Did Principal Spears return yet?" I barked into the phone.

"Um, yes. He arrived a few moments ago. May I ask who's calling?" she stammered.

"Zaydee Lansing. Transfer me," I commanded.

"Please hold," she said quietly. The sound of the 'on hold' music came over the speaker and I felt like punching the wall. I hated 'on hold' music, specifically more so when I had something important to say.

"Zaydee?" Garrett asked, in surprise.

"What the fuck was that? At my grandfather's funeral? Why did you do that?" I yelled into the phone.

"I'm not going to speak to you if you

insist on yelling."

The line clicked dead and I stared at the phone. *Did he really just hang up on me?* I was outraged and called the school back almost immediately.

"Rockford Hi--"

"Put Spears back on the phone," I said, cutting her off.

"I'm sorry, but he's not accepting any more phone calls today. May I take a message?" she asked brightly.

I slammed the phone down and got to my feet. If he wasn't taking my phone calls, then he could tell me exactly what he had been trying to accomplish in person.

Thirty minutes later, I was driving past the security post after identifying myself as a former student and went to the visitor parking lot he had directed me toward.

I pulled off the back of the visitor sticker he gave to me and jumped out of the truck, still dressed in my funeral clothes. I walked purposefully through the double doors and toward the administration office.

When I walked in, I saw that he was standing behind the secretary who had been playing devil's advocate with a file open.

"May I help you?" she asked, glancing up at me.

I locked eyes with Garrett, who flipped the file closed with the flick of a wrist. The look on my face must have been one of absolute rage because he chuckled and motioned for me to follow him into his office.

"If you start yelling, she'll call the police. Not because I've told her to, but because we have to protect our students," he said, closing the door behind me.

I stood behind the chair that was across from his desk, watching him as he dropped the file down and sat. He leaned back, crossed his arms behind his head, and gave me a stern look.

"Now, if you can talk to me like an adult, I have no issues having this conversation. The moment you raise your voice, Zaydee, we're done."

I began to drum my fingers on the chair and stared at him. I had to calm myself down before I spoke, otherwise he'd kick me out and I'd be escorted off of school property. Not exactly something I wanted to experience the same day as burying my grandfather.

"Why did you do that, Garrett?" I asked as calmly as I could.

"Because it was the best time to do it," he replied simply. "Frances is the reason that Scott is still in the family and he's also the reason you came back."

"I'm not staying. I have a home in Florida and I plan on going back there. You need to forget whatever you seem to think is going to happen here," I replied with a laugh.

Garrett leaned forward in his chair and clasped his hands on his desk. It was obvious that my laughter had pissed him off, because he turned an angry shade of red. I waited for him to flip out on me, but he didn't. Instead, he looked down for a moment, cleared his throat, and sighed.

"Sit down, Zaydee. You're making me nervous."

"There's nothing to be nervous about. I'm not staying. I'm happy that my grandparents were kind enough to give the kid a good home and keep him close, but I'm also angry. Angry that everyone seemed to know but me. Angry that there's fourteen years just sitting there that I'll never get back. Angry that I don't even want to try to make up for lost time," I replied, my voice starting to crack. "He's better off without me. Everyone here is. I only end up fucking everything and everyone over. Why should I try to step in now and make it right, when I wasn't even given a chance to make it work?"

"Because you owe yourself some happiness," he replied softly.

I let out a loud laugh. Happiness? Didn't he know that I was the perpetual sad girl? The girl that knew that happiness didn't come to everyone and I had resigned myself to that? That I was "happiest" being alone in my home in Florida where no one knew who I was?

"I'm my best self when I'm alone," I replied coldly. "You have a wonderful life now. You won't have to worry about me bothering you again."

"Would it change anything if I told you that I still love you?" he asked.

"You don't love me," I scoffed. "We had a stupid fling. You knocked me up, broke my heart, and the family kept it all a secret from me. I've had more than enough of Los Angeles to last me a lifetime."

"I gave up my entire life to be with you! My family! My home! Everything I ever knew was turned upside down the first time you kissed me! Do you really think that my feelings have just gone away?" he asked incredulously.

That simple plea from him put an idea in my head. If Garrett *really* loved me and wanted us to be together again, then I could make him prove it in more ways than one.

"Look, I have to go. I want to be alone for the rest of the day. Come by the Hilton on South Grand tomorrow and we can talk more about this when I have a clear head. I'm in room five-twenty-seven."

I looked at him and shook my head before I turned and walked out. The rest of the day would be mine. I'd take a nap, watch some television, and try to get this clusterfuck of a day out of my head.

Tomorrow would be different; with the dawning of a new day, I would put Garrett's declaration of love to the test.

Eleven

I was sitting on the carpeted floor of the hotel room the next morning watching The History Channel, when a knock came at the door. I had become so engrossed in the program on barbarians that I wasn't really aware of it until it came for a second time, and harder than before.

"Coming!" I called out, not moving from my spot. If it was that important to get into my room, whoever it was would be able to wait until a commercial came on. I pulled my legs underneath myself and leaned back against the edge of the bed, listening to the program expert when a voice rang out.

"Zaydee? It's Garrett."

I sighed and got to my feet. I went over to the door, unlocked it and pulled it open, keeping my eyes on the television the entire time. He walked into the room and I went back to my spot on the floor.

"Sit down somewhere. It's the History channel. You should like this," I said, waving at him absentmindedly.

Garrett chuckled and sat patiently on the edge of the bed. About six minutes later, the program breaked for a commercial, and I turned my head up toward him. He looked down at me with a smile and I shook my head.

"Shouldn't you be at school being official or something?" I asked.

"I called in sick. You told me you wanted me to meet you here, remember?" he replied.

"What can I say? I didn't think you'd show," I remarked with a shrug.

Garrett shook his head as he nudged me with his knee. I moved over on the carpet and he sat down next to me, bringing his knees up and resting his arms on them. He ran a hand quickly back through his hair and turned slightly toward me.

"I've been asking myself since you left yesterday if I should even show up. And now that I'm here, I'm asking myself why I'm sitting in the same room with you. Being around you brings back all of my old feelings; it makes everything feel like it might be okay again, but there's something really different about you, Zaydee."

"Adulthood," I replied dryly.

"That's not funny," he snapped.

I smirked. I couldn't really remember who had initiated our soiree when I was in school, but I do remember enjoying every time we were alone together. Of course, that could have just been the young, romantic girl in me with her first love, as opposed to the bitter, grown woman who refused to believe in love.

"Why am I here?" he asked, more calmly.

"Tell you when this is over," I replied, turning my attention toward the program as it came back from commercial break. Garrett sighed irritably, and I leaned over to rest my head on his shoulder.

We watched the remainder of the show in silence and at some point he managed to slip his arm around me. Being as engrossed in the program as I was, I hadn't noticed until it was over and went to get to my feet to turn off the television. After I shut it off, I went over to the window overlooking the city and smiled.

"It's been fourteen years, can you believe it?" I asked wistfully. "Fourteen years since I've been in this shithole of a city. If I said I missed it, I'd be lying. This place is full of bad memories for me. It seems to keep taking everything I love away too. There's so much pain here. How can you stand it?"

"I block it all out. Anything that's ever hurt me to think about, anything I've lost; I just push it all down into a place I can't reach. And quite honestly, Zaydee, it was working just fine until you showed back up," he admitted, shaking his head.

The smile on my lips widened a little. That was the thing with being damaged; no matter how hard you tried to keep it contained to just yourself, you always ended up hurting those around you.

"I'm going to Grandma's house today and though you might want to come," I said, finally answering his initial question.

"Yeah, I'd love to go," he replied as he got to his feet.

I tore my eyes away from the Los Angeles skyline and glanced at the clock near my bed. We still had a couple of hours before we had to get there, but I had already run out of things to say.

"What time is she expecting you?" he asked, coming over to the window.

"Eleven-ish."

"What's been your biggest heartbreak?" I asked, glancing up into

Garrett's eyes. He took a deep breath and let it out slowly. I wasn't exactly sure what his answer would be, but I knew I just wanted to know if someone else beside me could pinpoint where things went to hell in their life.

"I honestly don't think it was just one thing. I think it was a culmination of things here and there that eventually swelled into a volcano of piss and shit, and then boom; one day the pressure just boiled. That was also the same day I told Josie about us," he said with a chuckle.

"I really *am* sorry about that," I said softly.

Garrett shrugged as he sat down in the chair near the window. He didn't say anything more on that subject; almost like he didn't want to talk about it. I kind of got it though, because had he not kept me after school one day for being tardy to class, neither of us would be here having this damn conversation.

I glanced at him and tilted my head. Garrett's brown warm eyes were fixated on the skyline and I found myself slowly walking over the two or three steps toward him. He turned his attention to me and raised an eyebrow at my smile. Taking a deep breath, he moved the chair around so that he would be facing me completely. I filled the gap between us and put my hands on his shoulders, and watched a slow smile spread across his face as he gripped my hips.

"Remember how yesterday you said you gave up everything for me?" I asked, leaning down to graze his ear with my lips. He nodded and took in a shuddery breath. "How much more are you willing to give?"

"Anything I have left. Anything you want, Zaydee," he whispered as his voice started to tremble.

"Promise?" I asked, letting my lips travel to his neck.

"I promise."

I smiled deviously and straddled him in the chair. His breath caught in his throat because I had taken him off guard, but as I leaned down to kiss him, his hands firmly gripped my hips. I rocked ever so slightly as our tongues touched, and a sigh escaped my lips.

With as much as I hated to admit it to myself, the feeling I was getting from this kiss alone was enough to make me want to stay with him forever. I had never felt safer than when I was in his arms, no matter how forbidden it was at the time, it just always felt right. When I felt him push his hard cock up toward me, I pulled away from him and got off of his lap. It spooked me for some reason; no matter how good the kisses were, knowing that he wanted to be inside of me scared the shit out of me.

"I can't. Not yet," I whispered.

He let out a breath, pulled my face down to his and kissed me gently on the lips.

"I won't force you to do anything you're not ready for."

That's a first, I thought as I went back to my spot on the floor and went back to watching the History channel.

Twelve

By the time ten-thirty came around, we were walking toward his car. He offered to drive to Grandma's house and I accepted since I was pretty sure I wouldn't be worth much after our morning rendezvous. True, it hadn't been as much as he would've liked, but it was enough for now to keep him happy.

"Next time, we'll have to follow through on that," Garrett said as he pulled out of the parking lot.

"Who said there was going to be a next time?" I asked, with a playful laugh.

He glanced at me with a cocky smirk on his face. It had been damn obvious at this point that he had no intention of letting me leave so easily. It was probably even more obvious that I refused to back down on that.

Two weeks to sin with him was more than enough, and then I would go back home and erase the memory from my mind. I would act like this never happened and I would learn to stop looking at the fucking obituaries hoping for a familiar death.

Grandma's house wasn't far from the hotel. She had lived in Burbank ever since I could remember, and was too stubborn to leave it. Not that I thought anything was wrong with the place, I just knew that trying to convince her to move down to Florida with me would probably be out of the question. My heavy sigh got Garrett's attention, and I felt his hand suddenly on my leg.

"What's up?" he asked, keeping his eyes on the road.

"Nothing important," I replied quietly. I shifted in my seat in a way that it would knock his hand off and kept my eyes trained out of the passenger window all of the way to our destination. Garrett chuckled; he probably knew that us sharing the moment that we did before leaving meant little to nothing to me.

I'd never love him, and to be quite honest, I wasn't sure that I ever did. I never said it to him when I was younger and I wouldn't say it to him now. It's just how I was; the only person that had gotten an "I love you" out of me recently had been my grandfather, and he wasn't even alive to hear it.

"How are we presenting ourselves?" he asked, when he finally saw the city limit sign for Burbank.

I gave him a confused look and he shook his head.

"Never mind," he sighed.

Hm. Wonder what that's all about, I thought as I turned to look back out of the window again. I knew it wouldn't be long until we reached my grandparents' house and I didn't want to enter her home with any obvious tension between myself and Garrett.

"She said you can pull into her driveway," I told him, pointing as we approached the modest two-story home. I smiled at the yellow panels that lined the outside of the house, the wooden steps that I used to love sitting on as a child, and the tire swing that still hung from the lone maple tree in their front yard.

Smile still on my face, I went over to the swing, and gave the tire a gentle push. I found myself wondering if Scott had been on this swing at any point in his life, just once, and it made me turn away. It made me climb the stairs to my grandparents' house and ring the doorbell. There was a reason Grandma wanted me to come over today, and I wondered if it had anything to do with him.

I waited patiently until I heard the sound of Grandma's cane making thudding noises across the floor. She peeked through the old curtains hanging over the small side window and smiled when she saw me. A few seconds later, the front door was pulled open and she was holding an arm out toward me.

"Hi, Grandma," I greeted with a gentle hug.

"Oh, Zaydee. My darling Zaydee," she said happily. "I'm so glad you came."

"I never could say 'no' to you," I replied, pulling away. "Garrett came with me; I hope that's okay."

"Of course it is!" she exclaimed looking past me. "Come here and give me a hug, young man."

Garrett's face turned slightly red as he stepped forward and hugged Grandma. I smiled when I saw her hand grip the back of his shirt, before she pulled away and told us to come in. I waited until he walked past me so I could close and lock her door. Grandma and Grandpa always insisted that the deadbolt be locked first, then the doorknob. They said that way, if they ever forgot to lock the bottom one, the stronger of the two would always be set in place.

"Young man," I teased him quietly, as I caught up to them.

Garrett shook his head, an embarrassed grin spreading across his face as we sat down in the living room. I watched as he helped Grandma get comfortable in her chair before he came over and sat down next to me.

"Thank you," she said to him with a nod. "I put the tea kettle on, so hopefully it'll be ready soon."

"Thanks, Grandma," I said, clasping my hands on my lap. She smiled at me and set her cane next to her chair. I waited to see if she would say anything else, but she didn't. She just sat there smiling happily at me, stealing glances at Garrett when she thought he wasn't looking. I shook my head in amusement and decided to bring up the subject at hand.

"So, what's up, Grandma? Why did you want me to come by today?"

"Garrett, would you mind bringing me that box next to you?" Grandma asked him.

I glanced past him curiously as he grabbed a small, square, wooden box and handed it to Grandma. She asked him to wait while she opened it. I watched her pull out a few envelopes that were tied together, and told him to hand them to me. I held my hands out eagerly and began to untie the envelopes when her voice stopped me.

"Not now, Zaydee. When you're ready to go and leave again; that's when you open those," she said, in the sternest tone she could muster.

"Yes, Grandma."

I gave the envelopes to Garrett. If I held them, there would be more than a slight chance that I would wander off to open them and see what was inside.

"That was a brave thing you did yesterday," Grandma said, glancing at Garrett. "Larry may not have thought so, but I know that Frances would be proud of you, and that's all that matters."

"I thought he was going to die!" I exclaimed.

Garrett shrugged and leaned forward in his chair. "Our secret would have come out eventually, but I wanted to honor his wishes of not telling anyone while he was alive."

"You know, I was a young girl too when I met Frances. That man was the greatest and only love of my life. I miss him every day," she said, her voice cracking slightly.

The tea kettle started to whistle loudly as the water boiled. I got to my feet and went into the kitchen. I didn't want her to have to get up more than she had to, and I also didn't want her to see the tears that were starting to stream down my face. I used a dish towel to wipe my face clean, then used it to pick the kettle up off of the burner.

I wasn't crying because Grandma was; I had lost the empathy part of humanity a long time ago. I was crying because even though she had suffered such a devastating loss, she was trying to find the silver lining in the cloud. Her telling us that she met Grandpa when she was young wasn't a random fact that was thrown out lightly, and it wasn't trivia to hold on to for another day. It was her way to try to make us comfortable with whatever decision we made.

Goddamn it, Greta, I thought as I filled three small China cups with hot water, and dropped tea bags into each one.

If anything really was out in the universe, I could only hope that it would hear me begging for this visit to be as short as possible.

Thirteen

It was two o'clock in the afternoon by the time we left Grandma's. She sat in her chair and told us the story of her and Grandpa while we listened, drinking our tea.

Apparently, she had met him when she was fourteen years old and he was eighteen, but times were different then, as she put it. Also, she said she knew she wanted to marry him from the moment she saw him so no one could really tell her to stay away from him. I snuck glances at Garrett who had been smiling pleasantly as Grandma took us down memory lane, and I could only hope that he didn't think it was the same with us.

I had a moment of weakness earlier today, and I honestly didn't intend to repeat the mistake. It was what had gotten me into this clusterfuck of moving all the way to the other side of the United States to begin with.

It was also the reason I was an absentee mother, a recluse, a self-loather, and had such hatred for humanity. But as he drove me back to my hotel, I couldn't find it in me to crush his high spirits.

"I think we should go to Phoenix," Garrett said when he pulled into the hotel parking lot.

"For what?" I asked in confusion.

"To meet our son," he said, giving me a pointed look.

"Oh."

Oh! How could I forget already that he was in Phoenix?

"No," I replied thoughtfully, running my hands through my hair. "I've fucked up enough lives, I don't think it would do him any good for me to show up and shit on everything he knows. You should go, though! I think it would do you some good to meet him."

"Zaydee, you need to stop. You didn't fuck up anything or ruin anything that wasn't already meant to be ruined," he said as patiently as he could.

Truer words were never spoken, I thought with a soft chuckle.

"Let me know how he's doing, okay?" I said softly, as I leaned over and kissed him on his cheek. I reached into the back seat and retrieved the envelopes that Grandma had given to me in her home and pushed the door open.

I hopped out of his car and practically ran to the front door of the hotel, leaving Garrett calling my name from the driver's side window. I didn't turn around and I didn't stop. It would've made me weak enough to go with him to Phoenix and I didn't want to go. I didn't want to do that to an innocent kid who probably didn't know anything about me anyway.

I walked past the front desk and took

the stairs up to my room. I didn't feel like waiting for the elevator today either. I wanted to get to my room and make a very important phone call. Even though I wouldn't be going to actually *see* Scott, it didn't mean that I couldn't call and check on him.

When I got to my room it dawned on me that I didn't know Uncle Bill and Aunt Rose's phone number, so I would have to make a phone call I didn't want to in order to get the information.

Fuck. I'm really not in the mood for the third degree, I thought as I unhappily dialed my parents' phone number.

"Hello?"

It was Dad. *I knew I should have hung up after the second ring.*

"Hey," I said timidly.

He stayed quiet for a moment before pulling the phone away from his mouth and called out to my mother.

"Your daughter is on the phone!"

That stung. Like I had tripped a bee's nest and was being relentlessly attacked. But I took a deep breath and waited for Mom to come to the phone.

"Zaydee?"

"I was wondering if you had Uncle Bill's phone number," I said quietly.

Mom rattled off the number and I told her to wait so I could find a pen and piece of paper. When I was ready, I told her to go ahead. She gave it to me again and then was silent for a moment.

"Why are you calling Bill?" she asked curiously.

"Garrett and Grandma told me, Mom. I just ... I just want to make sure he's doing okay," I explained hesitantly.

"Send him our love."

Click.

The line went dead and I listened to the sound of the buzzing until it dropped off into silence. I sighed unhappily and thought of how much more damage had been done to my parents after they found out that Garrett was the one who had gotten me pregnant at such a young age.

I hung up the phone and looked down at the number I had scrawled onto the back of the envelope stack that Grandma had given me. I put the pen and the packet next to the phone and laid down to face the window. I wouldn't be able to call and check on him if I felt like a failure, so I decided to take a nap instead. Maybe by the time I woke up, I'd be brave enough to make that phone call.

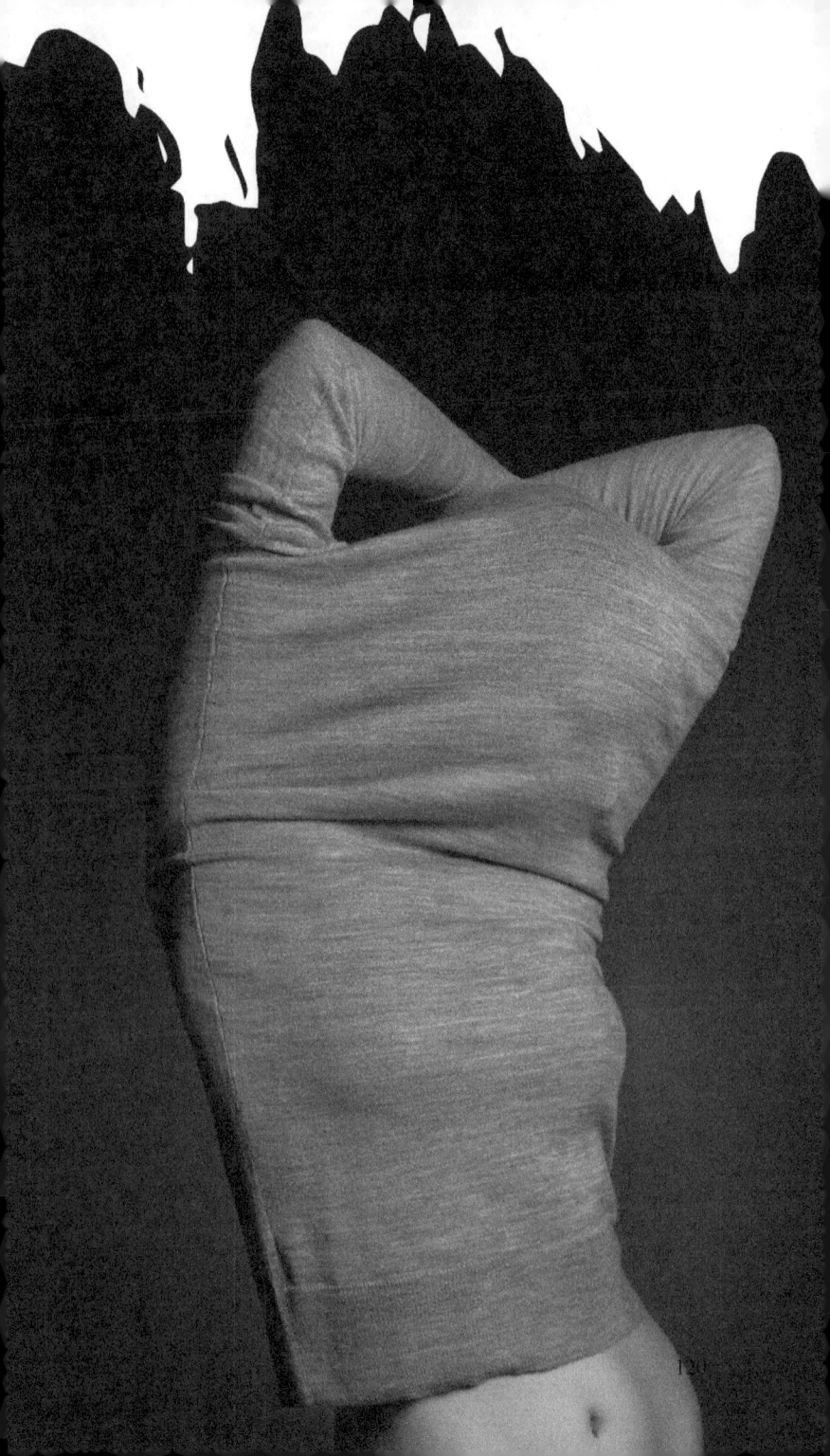

Fourteen

A few hours later, the sound of the phone ringing incessantly woke me from my sleep. My body was completely stiff, causing me to flinch when I stretched. I closed my eyes tightly for a moment before turning onto my back and looking up at the ceiling. I draped an arm across my forehead and turned my head slightly to the right, waiting for the ringing to stop. But since it didn't, I blindly started reaching toward it in frustration. I sighed heavily when I accidentally knocked the receiver onto the floor from its cradle and had to roll over the side of the bed to retrieve it.

"Hello?" I asked tiredly, when I finally put it to my ear.

"It's about goddamn time! I've been calling you for days," Garrett barked into the phone.

"What? I took a nap, don't be so dramatic," I said, rolling onto my back again.

"Zaydee, it's Sunday. How long did you plan on sleeping? Forever?" he asked angrily.

My eyes flew open and I sat up straight. There was no way in hell I had slept for two days. I had trouble sleeping full nights, let alone days at a time. I glanced around the room uneasily wondering what it was that had allowed me to sleep so peacefully. Whatever it was, I needed to buy one as soon as I got home, but there was nothing out of the ordinary that I could notice.

"Are you there?" Garrett asked, a little calmer.

"Yeah, sorry. What's up?" I asked, scooting myself back against the headboard. I reached for one of the large, fluffy pillows and put it behind me. I wanted to be comfortable enough, but not too comfortable. Falling asleep on the phone probably wouldn't impress him much.

"I'm calling to make sure you didn't change your mind. I told the school board that a family emergency came up and that I needed to take the week off. I'm leaving for Phoenix tomorrow morning."

I sighed. I understood his persistence, but he would just have to accept the fact that I wasn't going to bend on this. "No. Thank you. Just let me know how he is doing. That will be plenty for me."

"Alright. I'll call you as soon as I get there, okay?"

"Sure. Chances are I won't be leaving this room anyway," I replied with a tired chuckle.

He didn't hang up right away and neither did I. We were having that awkward listening to each other breathe moment again.

"I really did miss you," he said softly. "And I never stopped loving you. I couldn't; no matter how hard I tried to push you out of my mind, no matter how hard I tried to erase the memory of you in my heart, something inside of me wouldn't allow me to."

"Thanks," I replied quietly as I hung up the phone.

I wasn't used to 'I love yous' and genuine heart-felt emotion. I was used to twenty minute phone calls home to Grandpa Frances and nothing more. And even though he would end every phone call with an 'I love you, Zay', I never had it said to me the way that Garrett was saying it. I knew it was in a completely different way than Grandpa had always meant it, and somehow, it held almost as much meaning.

But I didn't have time for love. I didn't have time for much of anything these days that involved other people. I took a deep breath, slid down onto my back again and closed my eyes. I wasn't tired, but I needed a moment to detach myself from the feelings that were starting to grow inside of me for Garrett.

So as I laid there I did my best to crush the seed that was threatening to grow. I pushed it into the dark place that my parents had spent years in. I would refuse to let it blossom, and because of it, I would be a better person.

Fifteen

Garrett

I was sitting in the middle seat of the three-row-center on the 747. I never cared for flying because of this very reason, but I wasn't going to make a fuss about it. I was already nervous enough with what I was doing and I didn't need to think about anything else. My focus was on Scott and Zaydee possibly having a phone conversation at the very least, but she seemed as stubborn as she was the day she first walked into my classroom.

I shifted uncomfortably in my seat. I hated thinking about that first time because it always made me hard, and it shouldn't. Something like that shouldn't excite me.

I waited until the sign giving the okay to remove our seat belts flashed and I excused myself from where I was sitting. The people on either side of me sighed as I got up, but I paid them no mind. The only thing I could think about was my first time with Zaydee, and I was going to need some privacy.

I walked to the back of the airplane and opened one of the bathroom doors. Putting my hands on either side of the aluminum sink, I looked at myself in the mirror. *What the fuck was wrong with me? Why couldn't I ever shake the memory?* No matter how hard I tried, no matter what I did, nothing would ever quell it.

I turned around, unzipped my jeans, and pulled out my hard cock. I spit in my palm and closed my eyes, gripping it firmly in my hand as the memory flooded my mind again.

I sighed as I graded Matt's paper. I couldn't understand how some of my brightest students did so horribly on their homework.

The sudden sound of someone popping bubblegum made me raise my eyes from my desk. It was Zaydee Lansing and she had finally decided to grace me with her presence.

"Even for detention you're late?" I asked sternly, glancing at the wall clock above the door.

She rolled her eyes and sighed loudly.

"Where do you want me to sit?"

"Your usual chair will do just fine," I remarked, shaking my head.

I waited until she was seated before I went back to grading my papers. I had already decided that her late appearance and less than stellar attitude had earned her another afternoon in that chair.

There was only five minutes of actual silence before she started fidgeting around at her desk, chair scraping on the tile floor. I rubbed my forehead irritably with my forefinger and thumb.

"Problem, Ms. Lansing?" I asked.

"No. Well. Yeah. Can I ask you something?" she said, leaning her arms onto her desk.

"What's on your mind?" I asked, dropping my pen and leaning back in my chair.

"What made you want to become a teacher?" she inquired curiously.

I raised an eyebrow at her. I wasn't sure if she really wanted to know or if she was just making conversation, but I decided to answer her anyway.

"I liked the idea of helping people. When I went to college, I looked at my options and still felt my love of history swelling in me, so that's why I chose that path. I guess it was just the notion of helping people better themselves," I replied thoughtfully.

"Oh."

"So, if you don't mind, I still have a stack of papers to grade," I said, pointing down at my desk.

"Sorry. I just hate it when it's quiet. I always feel so lonely," she replied softly.

I groaned inwardly. I'd just have to take these papers home and finish them there.

"Why were you late to class today, Zaydee?" I asked.

She shifted uncomfortably in her chair. I could tell she didn't want to tell me, but I just wanted to know if she had a valid excuse and I could let her go home early.

"After gym class, I was in the showers and Marnie and her friends decided it would be funny to grab my bra and yell out the size to everyone. I was so embarrassed that I waited in the shower until all of the girls left. I'm sorry," she said quietly.

"Teenagers can be so cruel to each other," I remarked, shaking my head. "I wish you would've just told me that. I would've excused you for being tardy."

She shrugged and looked down at her feet. Her demeanor seemed to have changed, *but I couldn't quite tell in which direction until she spoke up again.*

"Yeah, but then we wouldn't have a chance to hang out alone together," she said shyly.

Huh, wonder what the hell that's supposed to mean, *I thought to myself.*

"Mr. S, can I tell you something?" she continued.

"Of course you can."

I watched Zaydee get up from her chair and walk over to the side of my desk. She let a hand fall on the pen I had been using to grade the homework papers, then raised her eyes to meet mine.

"I like you."

"I like you too, Zaydee. You're one of my best students," I replied fondly.

"No. I mean ... I like you," she said.

My hands started to shake at her confession. I had never had this situation happen with a student before, and I knew I had to tread carefully. I didn't want to hurt her feelings and I didn't want her to think anything would happen between us.

"Don't be shy; I've seen the way you look at me in class when you think I'm not looking. It's okay for us to like each other," she said, running a hand lightly up my arm.

"Zaydee. I'm your teacher," I said, emphasizing the last word. "You're my student, but that's it."

"It doesn't have to be that way. I was hoping you'd keep me after school eventually, and today just happened to work out in my favor. Do you think I'm pretty, Mr. S?" she asked, her hand resting on my shoulder.

Truth be told, I thought she was absolutely beautiful. She had the body of a grown woman; something my wife seemed to be lacking and even though I wouldn't admit it to her; I did sometimes look at her with thoughts that shouldn't have been running through my head.

I inhaled sharply as she pushed the papers out of the way and sat down on my desk in front of me. The look in her eyes told me what she wanted, and I knew my eyes were reflecting hers.

"We'll get caught," I whispered.

She smiled and got off of the desk, walked over to the door, and locked it. Then she went to the back of my classroom and rolled one of my mobile blackboards toward the door, blocking the small window view. Zaydee walked back toward me and went back to her spot on the desk.

"Do you think I'm pretty?" she asked again.

"No. I think you're fucking beautiful," I replied, my voice thick with desire as I leaned forward and pulled her on top of me.

She let out a surprised squeal that I stopped by pressing my lips against hers. Her clumsy response told me that it was her first kiss, but I had every intention of being patient with her. I wanted her more desperately than I *wanted anyone else in my life. Perhaps it was the thrill of being caught, or perhaps it was the thrill of being with a student, but either way I knew I wouldn't let her leave this room until I had fucked her properly.*

She pulled away from me long enough to take her shirt off. When she tried to kiss me again, I held her back for a moment to look at her full breasts and felt myself becoming hard.

I had never needed Josie the way I needed Zaydee. What I felt inside of me in this moment; it felt like my soul had been set on fire. Like everything I never knew I needed, everything I had denied myself, was finally sitting in front of me.

As I sat there taking her beautiful body in, I found myself wondering if the fire inside of me was what true love was supposed to feel like. With a deep breath, I looked up into her gray eyes and gave her another chance to walk away from it, from me.

"Are you sure you want this?" I asked her.

"Yes."

That was all I needed to hear. I kept one hand on her side, and used the other to slide her bra down, exposing her already hard nipples, and took one into my mouth. The way she wriggled on my lap as I sucked on it only made me harder.

I moved from one to the other, sucking and licking more feverishly than I did with the last, her moans making me want to rip her clothes off. But I was determined to take my time, because if I was her first kiss, then I knew I would also be her first fuck, and I wanted her to enjoy it. It meant she would come back for more.

"Up you go," I said softly, using my strength to place her on the desk. She smiled nervously at me as I pulled off her denim shorts. Once they were on the floor, I gently ran my hand over her black cotton panties, reveling in how wet I had already made her.

I pulled my chair forward and continued rubbing my hand gently over her panties. I wanted to taste her more than anything, but I always believed that teasing was just as sensual as the act itself.

It took everything I had to not slip my fingers inside of her. I didn't want to pluck her flower that way. I wanted her to feel me inside of her, I wanted it to be so intimate that she would beg me for more, and by God I would give it to her whenever she wanted.

But first ...

I moved her panties to the side exposing the small tuft of hair on her already glistening opening and smiled. I hated that Josie shaved everything off; it made me feel weird when we had sex. Zaydee, probably because she was so young, hadn't shaved anything and it only served to make me more excited.

I leaned forward and used the tip of my tongue to gently part her pussy lips. She groaned softly and grabbed the back of my hair. I chuckled slightly as I slid my tongue up and down a few times, intensifying the moment before I moved to her clit. Zaydee took a deep breath and formed a fist around my hair as I licked at her.

I could almost swear that she tasted like the sweetest honey in the world; freshly harvested from a bee's nest and made especially for me. I dug my hands into her hips as I continued moving my tongue against her until she came. It didn't take long for that to happen and again, I found myself feeling pleased.

I got to my feet and unzipped my pants. I let them fall around my ankles and my boxers followed as I guided the head of my cock toward her soaking wet hole.

"I'll go slow. It hurts the first time," I promised in heavy breaths as I pulled her ass down toward the edge of the desk. "Are you ready?"

She nodded, her eyes clouded over with a look that told me that she was just as lost in our moment as I was. A look that told me that I wasn't doing anything wrong, because she wanted it just as badly as I did.

As gently as I could, I started to push my length inside of her. She closed her eyes tightly and gripped my wrists as I continued my movements until I felt a warm rush go over my cock. It was done; the hardest part, the part I honestly didn't know if I would follow through with was over. Zaydee wasn't a virgin anymore and that meant she was mine now, just as much as I was hers.

I kept my rhythm gentle and slow, moving in and out of her as gracefully as I could, when what I really wanted was to fuck viciously. But I told myself that there would be time for that. This wouldn't be the last time that I had this beautiful fucking creature on my cock, and next time I would fuck her the way I wanted to.

"Fuck" I groaned through grit teeth, shooting my cum onto the bathroom wall across from me. I took a few steadying deep breaths and grabbed some tissue to clean myself off before washing my hands. I grabbed more and let some warm water run over it before I cleaned the wall, chuckling at what I had just done.

Maybe Zaydee didn't love me the way I loved her anymore, but I would always have the memories of when she did.

I flushed the used tissues down the toilet and went back to my chair. Stretching my legs out in front of me, I leaned the chair back as far as I could and decided to sleep the rest of the way to Phoenix.

Sixteen

Garrett

I quickly realized the flaw in my plan when I landed at Phoenix Sky Harbor International Airport. I didn't know what Bill or Rose looked like, so finding them here was going to be like finding a needle in a haystack.

The only thing I had to go on was what Greta had told me. They were related to Zaydee on her father's side and she looked a little bit like her Uncle Bill.

I skipped baggage claim, because the only bag I had was carried onto the plane. I didn't plan on staying long enough to need luggage. I just wanted to meet him and go back home to Zaydee. I went over to the escalator and nervously gripped the sliding railing.

Scott was more than just my son; he was a miracle born of a damaged lust. Josie had never been able to have kids, having had some kind of condition that left her with a one percent chance of ever conceiving. I wanted desperately to be a father, but no matter how hard we tried, it just never happened.

When Zaydee told me she was pregnant, I was ecstatic. I held it inside because she looked absolutely terrified, but I had every intention of being a father to our child. Her parents took fourteen years of a dream I'd had for so long and shattered it. Now I had a chance to make up for lost time and I would do my best to make him understand that we both loved him. I hoped Bill and Rose had explained the situation to him, and if they hadn't, then I would. I didn't want him to think that he had been abandoned by his parents.

After I got to the bottom, I stepped off and took a deep breath. I glanced around the large airport lobby to see if anyone around me resembled Zaydee. I didn't have to look for long though, because a tall, middle-aged man with a thick black mustache with a tiny woman by his side walked over to me and held his hand out.

"You're Garrett, aren't you?" he asked, with a kind smile.

"Bill?" I asked, shaking his hand firmly.

"Oh my God. He looked just like him," the woman who I assumed to be Rose, said quietly, nudging Bill.

"This is Rose, my wife," he said, confirming my thoughts and nodding at her. I smiled as she stepped forward and gave me a friendly hug, which I returned.

"Come on, our car is in the parking garage. Did you have a good flight?" Bill asked, leading the way down the large hallway.

I confirmed that I did and we made small talk all the way to his car. I kept a smile on my face and interest in my eyes, but I was honestly disappointed that they hadn't brought Scott with them. I kind of wanted to have one of those airport scenes that you see in the movies; the kind when you see someone you love and you run and embrace each other, while everyone around you starts to cheer.

Once in the parking lot, we took the elevator to the third floor in silence. I leaned against the back wall and stared up at the numbers as they ticked by, Bill cleared his throat a couple of times, and I felt Rose's eyes on me when she stole the occasional glance.

"Over here," Bill said once we were on the third floor of the parking garage. I followed as he and Rose led the way to an old beige-colored Volvo with a couple of dents in the side. He used a remote control attached to his keychain to unlock all of the doors and I slid into the backseat.

"Is your home very far from here?" I asked.

Bill shook his head slightly, "About half an hour, depending on traffic."

"Oh; and um, Scott? Is he there?" I asked nervously.

Rose put a hand on Bill's arm before she turned and looked at me with an emotion I couldn't quite read. She realized I couldn't understand what her face was trying to tell me, so she nodded before turning back around in her seat again. I decided it was better not to ask any more questions about him, so Bill and I bantered a bit about what there was to do in Phoenix, our favorite sports teams, and how long I had been in the education profession.

Thirty painful minutes later he was pulling into the driveway of a split-level home with a tire swing hanging from a tree in the front. I was starting to believe that was a family trait and wondered if Zaydee would have insisted on one, had we had the chance to keep him.

Probably, I thought with a smile.

Bill and Rose quietly got out of their respective sides of the car with me following. I walked up the splintered wooden steps close behind them and waited while Bill unlocked the front door and stepped back to let Rose in. I waited until he went in, then followed, closing the door behind me. My hands were starting to sweat and my legs were a bit shaky; I was honest to God terrified of meeting my son. What if I wasn't what he expected? What if he hated me for being absent for the first fourteen years of his life? What if he wanted Zaydee instead of me?

Maybe I should have waited until she was willing to come, I thought nervously as they led me into a den.

"I thought you'd like to look around in here, first," Bill said, sliding his hands into his pockets. "This is where we keep most of the family pictures and he's in almost all of them."

I cleared my throat and nervously started looking at the pictures. They seemed to be in chronological order, from when he was a small baby up until what age he would be now; around fourteen. I understood the haunted look on Rose's face when I first met them in the airport lobby. Looking at Scott really was like looking at a younger version of myself. The only traces of Zaydee I could see, was the progressive sadness in his eyes the older he grew.

The sudden thud of a glass being set on the wooden desk behind me got my attention. I turned slightly and saw that Bill had set down two square glasses and was currently filling them halfway with Scotch Whiskey.

"He was a great kid," he said, coming over and handing me one of the glasses. He took a drink of his as he looked at the pictures mounted on the wall. "He may have looked like you, but he was just like Zaydee. He loved Frances most of all and that tire swing out in the front yard," he said with a sigh.

"Was? Isn't he still?" I asked, in confusion.

Bill chuckled softly. "Scott was a manic depressive like Zaydee. It's hereditary, you know? Getting him to take his medication was always a hellacious fight. Garrett, I think it would be best if you took a seat."

I gave him a sidelong glance. Something about the way he said that told me that the rest of this visit wasn't going to be what I was expecting. I went over to the small leather two-seater couch and sat down. I leaned forward and held my glass of liquor tightly in my hands waiting for him to speak. Bill lingered in front of the pictures for a moment longer before he went and sat down in the recliner almost directly across from me.

"Did Zaydee take it hard when Frances died?" Bill asked curiously.

"I couldn't tell you, honestly. She moved to Florida a long time ago and I didn't really see her until she came back for the services. I'm sure it hurt her, but she played the part of the rock for her family," I replied thoughtfully.

"Scott begged us to take him to see Frances when we found out he was terminal. It took me a little while to scrape the money together, but we got him out there. I thought it would have been good for him, you know? To be able to see the man that he loved the most one more time before he died," Bill said, shaking his head.

"Bill. I'm starting to get a little worried here," I said, rubbing my forehead. "Where exactly is my son?"

He got to his feet and retrieved the bottle, topped off his glass, then came over and topped off mine. He sat down again with a heavy sigh and looked at me before he nodded.

"Rose! Can you bring Scott in please?" he called out.

I drank down the rest of the glass in one gulp and got to my feet. I faced the door waiting for Rose to walk in with Scott, but I wasn't expecting her to walk in with him like this. I wavered on my feet slightly and landed on my ass in the chair. The glass fell from my hand and bounced on the carpeted floor as Rose came over and handed what looked like a small, decorative vase to me.

"I'm so sorry," she said quietly as she handed it to me. "He couldn't take it when he finally realized that Frances was going to die. When we got back, he went into his bedroom and hung himself."

Seventeen

Zaydee

It was late Monday morning and I was sitting on the freshly restored green grass at Saint Raphael's Cemetery. Grandpa didn't have a headstone yet, but I managed to find him again after some driving around.

I figured by this point Garrett was most likely sitting around with Scott, so I wanted to be near someone I loved too.

I had my legs crossed underneath me and the envelopes that Grandma had given me were sitting on my lap. I still hadn't opened them, and even though she told me to wait until I got back home to read them, I wanted to read them with my grandfather nearby. Something told me that I might need his strength and this was the closest I could get to feeling it anymore.

"How's it going, Grandpa?" I asked softly.

The first envelope held a short note from Grandma.

Dearest Zaydee,

What you are going to discover in these letters may be difficult for you, but I know that you are strong enough to cope with it. Please know that I'm here for you if you need me.

Love,

Grandma Greta

I pursed my lips as I set the note down on one side of me and the envelope on the other. I didn't know what secrets the other envelopes held, but I was going to read them, no matter how bad the feeling was in the pit of my stomach.

I took a deep breath and picked up the second envelope. I smiled as tears brimmed in my eyes. I'd know Grandpa's writing anywhere, the way he wrote the Z in my name was artistic and always stood out to me. I pulled the letter out of the envelope, cleared my throat, and blinked back the tears as I read his letter to me. The way he addressed me in the letter made me laugh softly; he almost always called me Zaydee Gray because of my eyes. No one in my family had eyes the same color as mine.

Zaydee Gray,

You're reading this because I'm gone now.

I'm sorry I didn't tell you that I was sick; I didn't want you to worry about me. You always worried too much, even when you were a little girl. Rita took good care of me and so did Greta, but there's something that's been weighing on me heavily. Something I know I should have told you when it happened.

Your son Scott; Greta and I adopted him and gave him to Bill and Rose to raise. I felt it was best to keep him in the family. We all did our best and hope that when you meet him, you'll be as proud of him as I was.

All My Love,

Frances Lettsworth

"Thanks, Grandpa," I whispered, putting his note down on top of Grandma's and his envelope to the other side. I sighed and looked down at where he was resting beneath me, another sad smile curving the edges of my lips. I never did meet a man as great as my grandfather, and I was sure I never would.

I was okay with that. Some people in this world weren't meant for happiness and true love and I didn't mind being one of them.

I took a deep breath and raised my face to the warm sun for a moment. I felt like he was there with me. Standing over me as I read these letters, to make sure I was okay. With a sniffle, I moved onto the next envelope, only this one didn't house a letter or a note; inside of this one were pictures.

Pictures of a newborn in my grandfather's arms, being held in the hospital nursery. Pictures of an infant learning to stand with a big smile on his face. The more the pictures progressed in age, the more I saw that he looked like Garrett. However, when I started to get to what I assumed to be Scott's teenage years, the more his expression started to look like mine. Stoic, unhappy, and distant.

"It'll be okay," I said softly to the last picture of my son. "It always turns out okay in the end."

I set his pictures down on top of Grandma and Grandpa's letters and looked at the last envelope that was sitting on the grass. I didn't recognize the handwriting or the sentiment scrawled across the front. It wasn't something I had been given the chance to do and I still wasn't sure that I deserved the title. But there it was; the one word that would always remind me of how deeply scars truly run.

'Mom'

My lower lip trembled and my hands began to shake. Did I really want to read this? Did he really think of me as his mother even though he had never met me and I never had a chance to hold him?

I closed my eyes for a moment and blindly reached for the letter. It was amazing how something as light as a piece of paper could feel like the heaviest stone in the world. Like an anchor that was slowly dragging my heart down to the depths of the ocean, threatening to crush me with the pressure of all of my past misdeeds.

Don't be a pussy; open the letter, Zaydee.

I ripped the back of the sealed envelope away and opened the letter. There it was again; the first word in the letter was addressed to *Mom*.

Mom,

Gramps told me everything. He told me how sad you were that you weren't able to keep me and how alone you felt when Dad turned his back on you. I can forgive you for not physically being in my life because you didn't have a choice. What I can't forgive you for is never picking up the phone and calling me. I can't tell you how many times I wanted to hear your voice when I felt like everything was crumbling around me. I can't tell you how hard it is knowing what I'm going to do and never knowing if you honestly loved me.

Gramps is sick. I hated seeing him like that and I don't think I can do this anymore if he's not here.

I'm sorry.

I love you and I hope that you love me too.

Scott

p.s. Don't be sad. You didn't do anything wrong.

***

      Hours later and the sun was starting to set over the horizon somewhere behind me. I was still sitting at Grandpa's grave, trying to fully understand what I had just read. If it was what I had assumed it to be, then Garrett must have found out by now too. I didn't know if I should cry and I didn't know if it hurt me yet, because I didn't know *him.* What I did know was, even without being in his life I had failed him; he hadn't stood a chance with me or without me, and no matter what he said, it was most definitely my fault.

But the fault wasn't mine alone, and I wouldn't bear what should have been the heartbreak of this by myself.

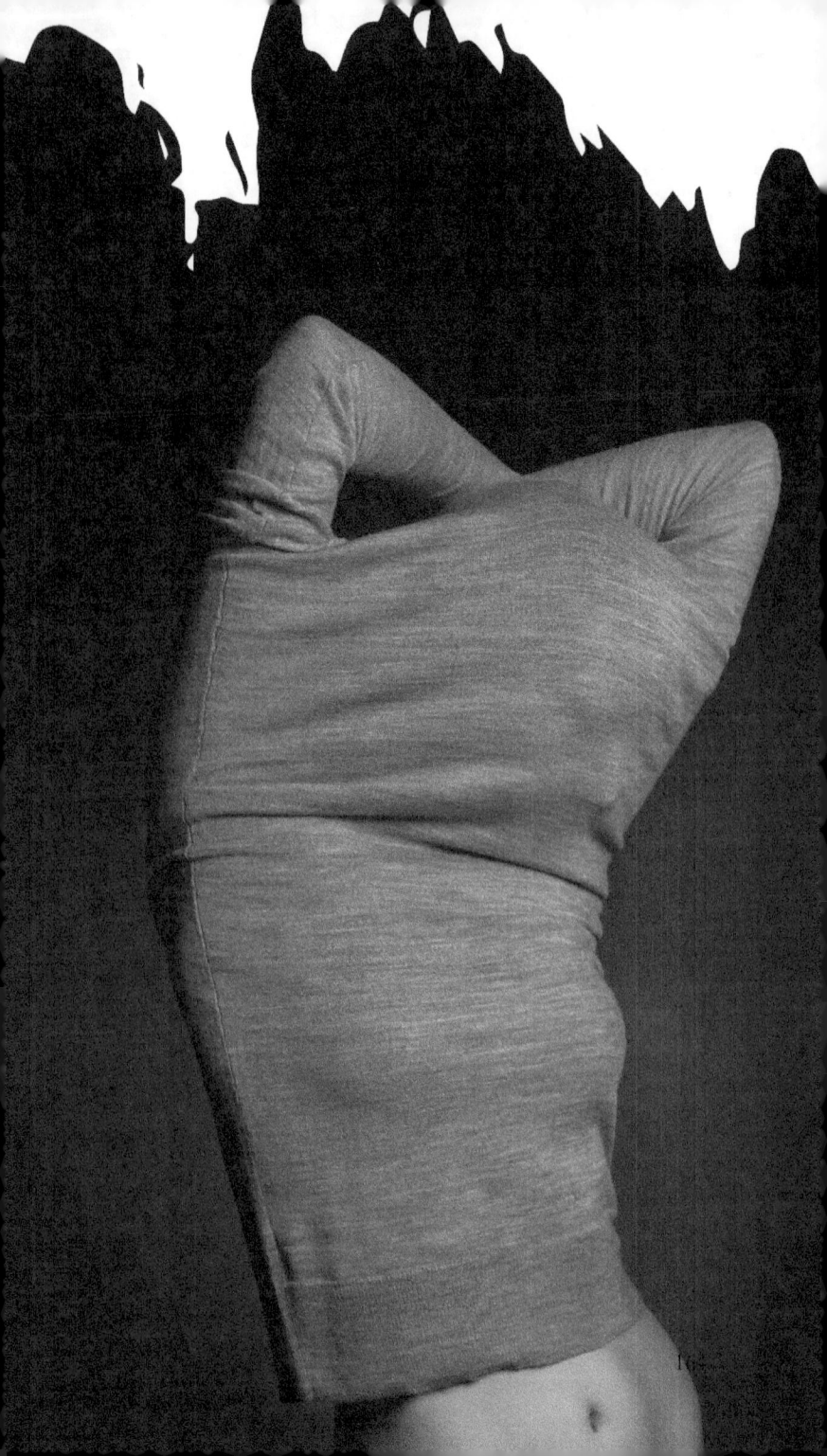

Eighteen

(Tuesday)

I was driving to the airport with all of my bags
in the backseat of the rental a week and a half
ahead of schedule, because I knew that it was
definitely time to go home. I had decided to
stop by Rockford High and leave a copy of
Scott's letter with Garrett's secretary on my
way toward LAX. It cost me a fortune to
switch the tickets around, but I didn't want to
be in Los Angeles anymore. This really was the
one place that seemed to continually break
me the longer I stayed.

I knew I would never have another
reason to come back to this place, and it
made me feel a little less broken. As I pulled
onto the highway I decided to turn on the

local rock station. I needed noise to fill the short drive to LAX, or else my own thoughts would consume me and it would drive me crazy. In my heart I knew I wouldn't have time for torturous thoughts; not now at least. That would have to wait until I got home.

I drummed my fingers on the steering wheel to the beat of the music and glanced up to see the LAX signs starting to appear. I sighed and glanced at the letters, then raised the volume of the radio and gripped the steering wheel so tightly that my knuckles were starting to turn white.

Easy, Zaydee, I told myself. *Deep breaths will keep the path clear and you need to see now more than ever.*

Three more miles and the highway opened into the huge airport parking lot. I drove past all of the airlines that were sectioned off for easy arrival and departures, and went straight toward the garage I had gotten the rental from. I wasn't exactly sure where I was going to leave it, but I figured as long as it was close to where I got it from then it should be okay.

I pulled into an empty spot on the third level and reached over for the stack of letters. I glanced in the backseat and reached for my carry-on bag, so I could put the envelopes in it. I didn't want to lose any of them, because they would be the best way to explain everything that I was going to do. Forcing a smile onto my face, I dragged my luggage behind me as I walked over to the rental car attendant in the small booth he was sitting in.

"One moment while I look the car over, please," he said pleasantly, walking past me with a clipboard in his hand.

I waited, the envelopes boring a hole through my bag and onto my hip, while he looked over the truck with a fine-tooth comb. When he was satisfied that no damage had been done to it, he had me sign the clipboard attesting to that fact, then let me go on my way.

I glanced at the clock mounted in his small booth and realized that if I didn't get a move on, I would most likely miss my plane. All of the damn daydreaming in the car had made me lose time, and I hadn't realized it until now.

I hoisted my baggage onto my back and ran down the stairs as quickly as I could, readjusting them when I reached the ground level. I knew that airport security wouldn't be too excited about me running through the airport, so I decided to power-walk my way to security after asking a guard where my gate would be.

I went through the same scrutinization I always did when I handed someone my identification before I was able to get through security. I knew I would have to pay extra at the gate for my bags, but I didn't care. I just wanted to get the fuck out of California and go home.

The lounge area was damn near packed by the time I got there, and I ended up sitting next to a man who seemed engrossed with his cell phone. I dropped my bags in front of the chair and fell into the seat, a relieved sigh escaping me before I glanced over at his phone.

My curiosity was soon satisfied when I saw that he had been texting someone named Jim, and the last text message received from him made me roll my eyes. Apparently, the man next to me was being told about a strip bar where all of the strippers had 'huge tits'" and would most likely let them do lines of cocaine off of them once he got to Miami.

This is gonna be a long flight, I thought with another deep sigh as I closed my eyes and waited for the flight attendant to start calling rows.

nineteen

(Wednesday)

It had just been my luck to have the seat next to the man with the *huge* plans once he got to his destination and I forced myself to sleep for the entire flight. Once I landed in Orlando International Airport though, I felt a sense of relief wash over me like a typhoon. I was happy to be back in a place where there was no heartbreak and no one would be able to give me any more shitty news. I was back in a place where things made sense, and no matter how bad things seemed, a bowl of ice cream, and a chick flick session would fix it all.

I went outside and waited in the valet line after retrieving my luggage from the baggage area. Ten minutes after handing my ticket to the same young man that I had generously tipped to keep my baby safe, he pulled around in my car. I threw my bags into the backseat and gave the car the once over, before handing him an extra one hundred dollar bill for a job well done.

Two hours later I was pulling into my driveway. I was finally home and I had zero plans on ever leaving again. I didn't care who died at this point; I had made it to the most important funeral I would ever have to go to, and that was enough for me.

After fidgeting with the locks on the front of my door, I stepped in and looked around happily. I let the bags drop on the side of the couch before I closed the door behind me and locked it firmly into place. I hadn't made it very far into the actual house when there was a knock on the door. With an eye roll and a groan, I turned around and went back to the door and pulled it open.

"Yes?" I asked the man who was standing in front of me, holding a flower arrangement.

"Ms. Lansing?" I nodded. "These are for you. I just need you to sign here, please," he said, placing the arrangement down and holding out a clipboard. I signed where he indicated and then took the arrangement from him.

"Have a good day, Miss!" he called out as he walked back down toward his waiting van.

I took the flowers straight into the kitchen and sat them down on the island. Not very many people knew where I lived now, and I was curious as to who would have sent them. Grabbing the card that had been attached, I flipped open the little envelope and smiled. I went back into the living room and fetched my cell phone, dropping down onto the couch and stretching my legs out, as I dialed. Three rings later and I was greeted by a familiar voice.

"Hey, Darlin'," he said happily.

"You've been living in Oklahoma for way too long," I replied with a laugh.

My cousin returned my laugh good-naturedly, "What's up, Zee?"

"I just got your flowers and I wanted to say thank you," I said.

"No problem. I told them to keep going back with them until you opened that damn door. It sucks about Frances; did you end up going back home?" he asked. I heard a dog barking in the background followed by a quiet shushing.

"Yeah; you didn't miss anything. Mom was a mess, Dad was trying to win the Father of the Year award, and Uncle Bill and Aunt Rose were part of the great family conspiracy," I replied dryly.

"What conspiracy?" he asked curiously.

"Remember when I got knocked up and they wouldn't let me keep the baby?" I paused for a moment. I had always been really close with him, so I knew I wouldn't have to sugarcoat my feelings about this, regardless of the fact that Bill and Rose were his parents.

"Yeah."

"Turns out Grandpa and Grandma adopted him. It was a boy they named Scott and Bill and Rose raised him, and all signs point to suicide on his end," I explained with a shrug. Not that he would be able to see it.

There was silence on the other end of the line. He had left when he was still a young man, so I knew that he couldn't have possibly known about his parents and my child. But the silence was still unusual for him. Almost as if he were trying to think of what to say without triggering anything inside of me. One of these reasons we were both so close was because we were both prone to fits of blind rage if pushed too far.

"Are you okay? Do you want me to come out there?" he asked quietly.

"I'll be fine. Don't waste your time worrying about me; it'll all be okay soon enough," I replied with a small chuckle.

"Anyway, I just wanted to say thanks for the flowers, Cowboy."

"You're welcome, Zaydee," he replied warmly, before we said our good-byes and hung up.

I let the phone drop onto the carpet next to me and draped an arm over my forehead. I was tired, but I didn't want to take a nap because all I'd really done the past few days was sleep. I could've unpacked my stuff, but I hated that even more than packing, so I decided to lounge around for a bit until I got some energy to do something; anything.

I thought of my cowboy cousin and how much I missed him. Maybe I should have told him to come see me after all, but I knew better. Something about him had always been unstable, so I believed that him being alone in rural Oklahoma was always best for him.

I pushed the thoughts of him out of my mind. With as much as I loved him, and with as much as it was nice to have family I could still say that about—besides Grandpa and Grandma–and I knew that I had to figure this out on my own.

Well, maybe not completely alone.

I leaned down and scooped my cell phone off the carpet. When I checked the battery life, I saw that it was almost dead, so I went over to my carry-on bag and fished around until I found the power cord. Once I had everything I needed I went back to the couch and unplugged the small lamp on the table at the end of the couch and plugged in my phone. I figured I could wait until it was fully charged before I made my phone call.

After all, there was only one person who would fully understand my internal torment right now and I didn't think it was fair for either of us to suffer this alone.

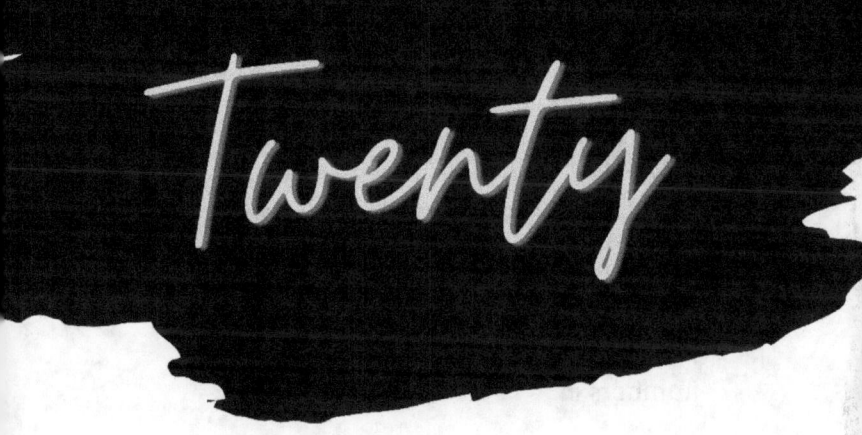

Twenty

(Thursday)

It was 12:01 in the morning and I had decided to stop flip-flopping with the phone call. The device had long since charged, but I didn't know if what I was intending would breed the intentions that I wanted, so I spent the rest of the day and the night sitting on it.

I had managed to make one phone call, but not the important one; not the one I needed that would help quell the pain. I took a deep breath and got up from the carpet of my bedroom floor that I had been sitting on, and walked over to the other side of the bed where my phone had been charging on the nightstand.

With unsteady hands, I brought the screen to life and plopped down on the edge of my bed. I glanced back at the nightstand and grabbed the paper that held the phone number on it, then used the light of the phone screen to read it and punch the numbers in.

After the fifth ring, I was ready to give up, but a froggy voice came onto the line.

"Hello?" he asked.

"Hey. Sorry I'm calling so late, but I can't sleep," I said softly.

"What time is it?" he asked.

"Past midnight. I'm sorry I woke you up, but I needed to talk to you."

"Zaydee, there's something you should know," he said in a slightly clearer voice.

"I already do know, Garrett," I replied with a sigh. "That's why I wanted to call you. You still have some time off this week, don't you?"

"Yeah," he responded with a heavy sigh of his own.

"Will you come see me? Please?"

"Text me your address. I'm still in Arizona, but I'll take the next flight out to you," he promised.

"Okay. Thank you. Sorry again for waking you up," I said quietly.

"It's okay. I'll see you soon," he said softly as he clicked off the line.

I waited about ten minutes before I sent him my address. There was something inside me, something that was once good and pure, something that *cared and* was trying to get me not to do this, but I pushed it away.

I wasn't pure and good; not anymore, and I knew I never would be again. I knew that the only way to end the pain of losing Scott, the little bit of pain that I felt, would be with Garrett. It was probably hurting him more than it hurt me because he couldn't understand that the boy was better off without us. He was better off dead. With as much as I hated to admit it to myself, he really was.

Once I got the response from Garrett that he had received my message, I shut my phone off, and put it back onto the charger before splaying onto my back on the bed. I wasn't sure when he would be arriving, whether it would be later today, or even tomorrow, but I had to make the most of what was yet to come.

***

It was noon when I finally woke up. I don't know how I managed to sleep for almost twelve hours, but I felt refreshed and more sure of myself. The doubt of what needed to happen was gone, and I found myself actually looking forward to Garrett's visit.

I got up and went into the bathroom, humming a happy tune to myself as I retrieved the toothpaste and my toothbrush. Running it under the water for a moment, I put a quarter sized amount of paste onto the bristles, before running it under the water again, then proceeded to brush my teeth.

I was still happily humming to myself and scrubbing my teeth when a knock came at my front door. I rolled my eyes and spit the paste into the sink, grabbed my small plastic cup, filled it with water, and swished. The knock came again, more persistent than the last time, and I spit the water into the sink before running the brush under It again and placing it in its holder. I quickly turned around and pulled a small washcloth out of the linen cabinet behind me to wipe my face, then tossed it into the hamper as I walked out of the bathroom.

I glanced at the time and sighed. It was quarter after twelve, I had woken up only moments ago, and it seemed that Garrett was already here. I knew it was him because I recognized the heavy-handed knock that mimicked the one from the hotel room door.

I stopped in front of the door and waited a few moments. I wanted him to knock again, for no other reason than to prove to me that he wanted to be inside with me. It would be a small consolation in the downfall that had been my life; to have someone who actually *wanted* to be in my presence.

I placed my hand on the doorknob and closed my eyes, waiting for the knock I knew would come again. Garrett had only let me down once in my life before, and I think that now that I was back in his, he would do his best to make it up to me for as long as he could.

"Zaydee?" his tired voice rang out, followed by the knock.

I smiled and closed my eyes for a moment before I pulled the door open. There he stood on the other side, a luggage bag hoisted over his shoulder and a decorative vase in his hands. His eyes were dim; as dim as I saw the world that night in the hospital and he looked like all he wanted to do was just lay down and sleep for the rest of his life.

"What's that?" I asked, stepping back and letting him walk in.

Garrett cleared his throat but didn't answer my question. Instead, he glanced around the living room before walking away from where I was standing. Curiosity would've made a normal person follow him to see what he was doing, but I was far from normal, so I went to the couch and turned the television on.

A few moments later he returned and sat at the other end of the couch, the vase still in his hands. I knew he wanted me to ask again, even though I had guessed full well what it was at this point. I assumed I should show some kind of sadness and pity, considering he had remembered to bring Scott with him, but I wasn't sure how to bring it up without sounding insensitive about it.

"How was Arizona?" I asked, my eyes on the screen as I started flipping through channels.

Garrett scoffed and put the vase on the living room table and turned to look at me. I didn't meet his eyes until I found the History Channel. The current program was something about archaeology in Ancient

Egypt. It seemed interesting enough to keep my attention away from the inevitable hurt I was supposed to be feeling.

"Bitter, to say the least," he finally said. "Your Uncle Bill and Aunt Rose seem like good people."

"Yeah, my favorite cousin is their son," I replied distractedly. *Wow, they were really advanced for their time,* I thought becoming engrossed in the program.

"And Scott is dead," he said bluntly.

"I know."

Garrett reached over and snatched the remote control from my hand in a quick motion and shut the television off. I looked at him in outrage but softened when I saw the angry tears streaming down his face.

"You *know*?" he repeated incredulously. "How long have you known? Did you know what I was walking into?"

"Not until you left," I admitted with a sigh. "That box Grandma gave you for me had some notes and letters in the envelopes. One had pictures too. Anyway, his suicide note was in one of them. At least that's what I think it was."

I jumped when he quickly got to his feet, swearing loudly. It was almost as if *I* had killed Scott and kept it a secret from him. But to be honest, had I known ahead of time, I still wouldn't have told him. I wouldn't want to kill his hope of maybe meeting him, and I think that finding out separately as opposed to together was better anyway.

Was I hurt by it? To some extent. Was I willing to show it? No, and he would have to accept it.

"Sit down and stop yelling," I said, suddenly developing a headache. I put my fingers to my temples and began to rub them in a circle, but Garrett was obviously far from done in his sudden rage.

"Zaydee, I refuse to believe that you aren't bothered by this. I refuse to believe that this doesn't hurt you as much as it hurts me. How can you sit there and act so coldly about it?"

I chuckled and shook my head, getting to my feet to face him.

"Because, *Principal Spears,* this should never have happened. If I hadn't been late to class that day and hadn't decided to try to fuck the sexy history teacher, we wouldn't have kept our little rendezvous going, I wouldn't have ended up pregnant and shunned, and we wouldn't have a dead child as a result. So, as you can see, I can't let something bother me that was never meant to be in the first place."

The anger left him almost immediately. He knew I was right, and I was willing to say what neither of us would. I never loved Garrett after my baby had been taken from me. I tried and he turned a cold shoulder to me when I needed him the most. My family shunned me, and the only person who ever understood me and gave a shit about me, lived hundreds of miles away.

To say I didn't have a chance at a meaningful life after that incident was beyond an understatement. Nothing he could say would break me now, and nothing he could put in front of me would make me feel something I never should have felt to begin with.

The only thing I wanted now was revenge for a life taken that was born out of ill intentions, desperation, and the need to feel loved.

He would learn to accept what I now wanted from him; he owed me for years of a stolen childhood I could never get back.

Twenty-One

(Friday Morning)

I allowed him the luxury of sleeping the rest of the day and majority of the night in my king-sized bed, while I stayed in the living room on the couch. For what I had planned for him, I admitted to myself that it was the least I could do; to let him have a small amount of comfort.

I woke up with a crick in my neck and a rage that was swelling my heart, easily masked by my day-to-day ability to blend in with the rest of humanity. Like the automated humanoid I had trained myself to be, I went into the kitchen and decided to make enough coffee for the both of us. I needed him alert and willing to fight for what he wanted.

Reaching into the kitchen cabinet, I retrieved two mugs and placed them on the counter before going over to the island in my kitchen and hopping onto one of the stools. As I sat there waiting, I tried to wrap my head around the fact that it had been a week since my grandfather had died, and all of the horrid feelings I had left behind in Los Angeles came back, washing over me like a torrential downpour of pain and regret.

With a quick glance toward the brewing coffee pot, I got up and decided to go to my room to retrieve my laptop. I quietly and slowly opened the door, so as to not disturb Garrett if he was still sleeping, which I saw that he still was. I pushed the door open halfway then slid into my room, found my laptop, and closed it quietly behind me as I went back into the living room and powered it on. I wasn't going to hunt for any obituaries; I had learned my lesson the last time. No, instead I was going to open a blank Word document and see if I could put my feelings down on paper, so to speak.

I knew that nothing I said would be as eloquent as what Scott had tried to put into words, but I would do my best. I would let anyone who had the heart to read it know that I had the best of intentions with what I was going to do. I wanted anyone who sat down to read it, know that even though things hadn't quite turned out as they should have, that I was finally happy and it was the best thing for everyone.

By the time I had filled about five document pages, I heard Garrett's shuffling feet as he entered the kitchen. The coffee had long been brewed, but I had become so engrossed in what I was doing that I hadn't moved. I wasn't even sure I had heard it finish, since I had somehow managed to desensitize myself to everything that *wasn't* what I had set my mind to do.

"Good morning," he said groggily as he opened the small glass jar that held the sugar. I immediately saved and closed the document before pulling the lid down on the laptop. I wasn't done yet but I couldn't let him see it until it was complete.

Gingerly, I dropped my chin into my hand and watched him scoop sugar into the beige, ceramic mug before pouring coffee into it, then going into the refrigerator for milk. I smiled when I knew he wasn't looking; it made me wonder how this tired man who had been through almost as much heartache as I had, could still function without forcing himself to be normal. Garrett Spears was an enigma, and with as much as I wanted to figure him out, I knew there wouldn't be enough time for that.

"Morning," I replied softly.

I watched his back as he raised the mug to his lips, and took a deep breath and a sip, before turning and coming to sit at the island with me. His eyes were still red, and I couldn't tell if it was because he had been crying again or if he was just tired.

"You okay?" I asked, running a hand back through his hair.

"No. But I'm not worried about me right now," he said, taking another sip then placing the mug down on the island top. His dim brown eyes searched mine seriously before he spoke again.

"Zaydee, I know that you're a tough woman; you always have been. But I need to make sure that you're okay before I leave and go back to L.A."

A smile danced across my lips again. Tough wasn't the word for what I was; empty, broken, damaged, and self-loathing were probably the words I would have chosen, but I wasn't going to worry him over something that wouldn't be a problem for much longer.

"I'm fine," I replied, putting a hand on top of his. "I hope you're not leaving any time soon though."

Garrett's eyes fell down to my hand for a moment. Almost as if he were deciding whether he should pull his hand away from mine, but ever since that first time in his classroom, I knew that my touch was something he always craved. Even when he shunned me and tried his best to pretend that I didn't exist, I knew.

"I'm scheduled to return to work on Monday," he reminded me, his eyes still on my hand. "But I can try to extend it and stay as long as you need me to. I won't ask you to come back to Los Angeles; I know what that would do to you psychologically."

"Have you ever heard the phrase 'you can't fix what isn't broken'? That's kind of where I am right now, only it would be more along the lines of 'you can't break what isn't meant to be fixed,'" I said, taking my hand off of his.

"Zaydee --"

"Stop," I said, cutting him off and holding up a hand. "I know what I am, Garrett. I know what's inside of my head every second of every minute of every day, and you don't. I know that you love me, but I can't say that back to you because I honestly believe myself to be incapable of loving anyone in that manner any more. Did I ever love you? Yes; at one point, I believe I did. Can I ever love you again? No, and it's not because of your abandoning me when I needed you, it's because of who I am."

He grunted and took another sip of his coffee before he got up from his stool, went over to the sink, and dumped it. The mug made a dull thunk noise as he dropped it into the sink, before gripping the edges of the counter with his hands. I could tell that he had a lot to say to me but didn't know how to say it. I assumed he wanted to plead a case for the theory of "us" and no matter how strong his emotion would be behind it, I wouldn't falter. I wouldn't let myself know heartache and loss again; I refused to allow it.

"Why am I here?" he asked quietly.

"Because I asked you to come," I answered, getting up from my stool and going over to him. I put my cheek against his back and rested my hands on hips. "I'm sorry that I can't and don't love you. I'm sorry that we can't go back to what we used to be, but you just being here with me makes me feel better about everything that's happened. Can that be enough for you?"

He didn't answer me, not with words. Instead he took another deep breath before he turned to face me. I crossed my arms over my chest and looked up into his eyes, wondering if they would ever shine with the beautiful light they once did. The same warm, shining, brown eyes that had taken my breath away when I first walked into his classroom.

"I guess it has to be," he finally said, letting out a sigh.

Placing my head on his chest and wrapping my arms around his waist, I made him a promise I intended on keeping.

"It's okay, Garrett. It'll all be over soon anyway."

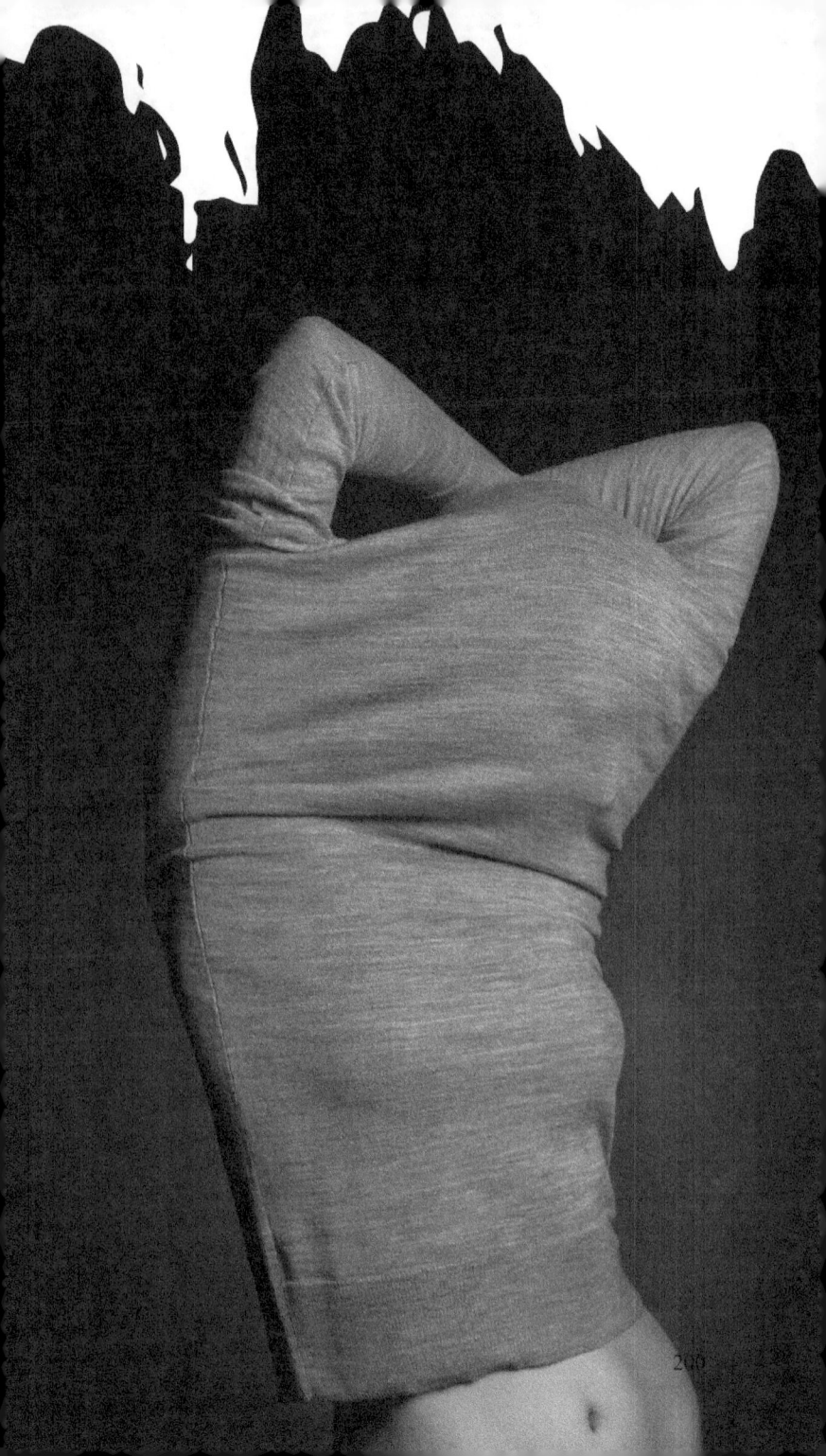

Twenty-Two

(Friday Evening)

What time is it? I wondered, craning my neck to look at the clock in the kitchen. If my eyes weren't deceiving me, it was 8pm and Garrett was still asleep on the couch. I hated to wake him up, but I knew that if I didn't start this now, I would never get it done.

"Hey," I said softly, leaning over and giving him a gentle poke in the side. "Garrett?"

He moaned quietly and rolled onto his other side, eyes still closed, and a foot still in dreamland.

"Garrett?" I asked a little louder, giving him a gentle shake. "Are you awake?"

He groaned loudly and rolled onto his back. I smiled; I couldn't help it. The way his hair sat messily on top of his head, so wild and free, was far from the kind of person I knew he was.

I gingerly placed a hand on his thigh and waited for him to open his eyes. It was something that made me feel somewhat loved, to know that a single touch from me could have so much power over him.

"I am now," he finally said, using one of his knuckles to rub his left eye.

"I think something about this house makes it easy to sleep for hours," I said in amusement.

Garrett sighed and let an arm rest across his forehead, blinked a few times, then cocked his head so he could look at me. His eyes smiled at me, but his lips couldn't form the sentiment that they shared. I wasn't upset with him for it, and I certainly wasn't angry. He was grieving a loss that should have been both of ours, but I had laid the burden of it on his shoulders, so he knew he would have to do it for me as well.

"How are you holding up?" he asked curiously.

"Fine," I replied, taking my hand away from his leg. "And you?"

He scoffed and brought himself up to a seated position. I pulled my legs up to my chest on the couch and wrapped my arms around them as I waited for him to respond.

"Fucked up," he replied honestly, running a hand irritably through his hair. "Not that you would know what that feels like."

I rested my head on top of my knees and looked at him for a moment. Garrett didn't know me; he didn't know what was inside of my head, and no matter how frustrated he was with me for not throwing myself on the floor and crying my eyes out, he couldn't possibly know the true depths of "fucked up" that was spiraling inside of me. It was like a giant sinkhole in the middle of the ocean that pulled at me every day, threatening to drag me to the darkest depths, and it was all I could do not to drown.

But today would be the first day since I started swimming near that sinkhole that I wouldn't fight its pull. I would welcome it, and I would let myself spiral down, just to see how far into the darkness I could go before I finally succumbed to the pressure caving in all around me. Until every dark thing that had ever run rampant in my mind finally took over and crushed me in its precious grip.

Would I survive the pull? I didn't know, and I had finally reached the point where I didn't care and hoped that it would be a beautiful demise; I hoped the intensity of it would make me smile one last time before I let it take me into the unknown.

But, first thing's first.

"Can I ask you something?" I said, turning my eyes away from him.

"Yeah," he replied tiredly.

"That first time. In your classroom? How did it happen? I can never remember," I admitted softly.

"What do you *think* happened?" he asked curiously.

I scoffed and got to my feet. I walked to the doorway that sat between the living room and the kitchen and leaned my back against it, letting my eyes wander toward the ceiling.

"I honestly don't know. I've spent most of my life thinking you forced yourself on me, but with as many times as you've told me you loved me in the past couple of weeks, something tells me that's not what happened."

"It's not!" he replied in shock. "Zaydee, I never forced you to do anything. *You* came on to *me* and I didn't stop it from happening. I know that I should have and this all never would have happened, but I couldn't resist you. You looked at me with such sad eyes, such heartbreak, and then all of a sudden you looked at me the way a grown woman would. You've always been... more developed than you should be and I lost myself in that lie. I saw you as a woman and not as a child and I... fuck. This is all my fault. All of it. I'm so sorry."

His voice cracked when his millionth apology left his lips, and I turned my face slightly to look at him. I pitied him for loving me as much as he did. I pitied him for thinking that telling me would change the kind of person I was. But most of all, I felt sorry for him because I knew how this had to end.

"Garrett? Remember how when we were going to Grandma's house? You said that the next time we would go through with what we started?" I asked.

He didn't verbally answer me, but he nodded his head slightly, using the back of his hand to wipe the tears from his face.

"Give me a few minutes," I said, walking away from the door frame and heading into my bedroom.

I didn't want to drag it out any longer than I had to, and I just wanted to leave him with a small ounce of happiness before I left. *I have to move faster,* I thought as I glanced at the time on the alarm clock on my nightstand. Friday would be over soon and I didn't want to wait another week.

I went to my walk-in closet and walked straight toward the back left corner. I pulled out a pretty black dress, held It up, and smiled. It was what I had worn the last time I saw my grandfather and it still fit me for the most part. I pulled off my clothes before slipping the dress over my body then went back to my bedroom. I went over to the entertainment stand that held a box of jewelry that belonged to Grandma when she was younger and pulled out a beautiful silver necklace. I wanted to look my best when I left, and one glance in the standing mirror mounted on the inside of the closet told me that I looked just fine.

I closed the closet doors and flipped the light off in my room. When I went back into the living room, I walked over to the smaller closet space I had in there and pulled out a pair of black flip-flops. Everything was ready; all I would have to do was slip them on then leave once I was done with Garrett.

I turned around to face him and smiled shyly. It was as sincere of a smile as I could muster, and for the briefest of moments, it looked like his eyes were shining again.

"Ready?" I asked softly.

"For what?" he asked, in confusion.

My smile deepened slightly as I walked over to him and straddled his lap.

"For me," I said softly as I gripped the sides of his face, leaned forward and kissed him as passionately as I could.

In no time, his hands were gripping my hips tightly as he returned my kiss, and I almost shivered when he sighed gently into my mouth. I reached down for his shirt, but before I could pull it out of his pants, he grabbed my hands by the wrists and pushed me back.

"No. This isn't right; not now," he said, his breath laboring slightly.

"This is your only chance, Garrett," I replied, trying to kiss him again.

"Zaydee, stop!" he shouted, shoving me off of his lap.

I hit my head on the coffee table and fell onto the carpet. I sat up with hand cradling my injury. I brought my hand forward and saw a small amount of blood on the tips of my fingers before I pushed myself to my feet.

"I didn't want to have to do it this way," I said quietly.

"I'm sorry. I didn't... I didn't mean for you to get hurt. Can I look at that, please?" he said, reaching for me.

I took a few unsteady steps backwards, before I went over to where my flip-flops were sitting and slid my feet into them.

"Zaydee, let me look at your head," he said again, getting to his feet.

"Stay away from me," I replied sharply.

I knew it wouldn't work. Trying to be normal was something that I had to work hard at, and the facade never lasted longer than mere moments.

I went into the kitchen to retrieve the last item I needed before I left. With an angry slam, the drawer I had opened clanked shut, the insides making a loud noise as the contents rattled around inside.

"Hey," he said, entering the kitchen. "Are you going to let me look at your head or am I going to have to strap you down and do it?"

I put the item I had come in to retrieve on top of the island and his face turned white. He held his hands up and took a step backward.

"Zaydee, what are you going to do with that?" he asked cautiously.

"Oh it's not for *you*," I replied in disgust.

"Then who's it for?" he asked nervously.

"Go get the vase," I commanded, nodding toward the living room.

"Give me the knife first," he said quietly. I could tell that he was mustering courage to come near me. *Me* of all people; Zaydee Lansing, the girl who had accomplished nothing in twenty-eight miserable years on the planet.

"Go get it!" I screamed, picking up the large, sharp kitchen knife.

Garrett licked his lips nervously, but finally nodded in agreement as he quickly left and reappeared with what was left of the only good thing I might have done.

I placed the knife down on the counter and held out my hands. Garrett handed me the vase and I smiled as I looked down at it. A sad smile, a smile that told me that I was doing the right thing. I took a deep breath and held what was left of my son closely to my chest, my eyes closed for a moment.

"I'm sorry," I whispered to Scott.

In quick movements, I placed the vase down on top of the island, pulled the lid off and looked at the ashes deep inside for a moment. Then I grabbed the knife and dragged it as deeply as I could across my throat. My hope was to get some of what was left of the last few moments of my life in with my son's ashes. In a sense, this way I would have finally been with him.

The feeling of the cool blade burned slightly and I had to tug it across after I somehow managed to get it stuck in the front of my neck.

I heard Garrett's horrified scream as I fell over, and I could feel the choking feeling take over me as the light from the world started fading again.

But it was over now; I could feel it as the cold washed over me. And I would look my best when I saw my grandfather, and possibly my son, for the first time.

Frances Lettsworth, aged eighty-four, the greatest man I had ever known, died on a Friday not seven days before. I could only hope he knew in his heart that I had done this for him.

Grab your FREE copy of What Lies Beneath by scanning here:

"The atmosphere is dark and ominous, and there's seemingly no escape from the monster. But the question is, who is the real monster?" — USA Today Bestselling Author Ellie Midwood

ABOUT THE AUTHOR

Yolanda Olson is a USA Today Bestselling and award-winning author. Born and raised in Bridgeport, CT where she currently resides, she usually spends her time watching her favorite channel, Investigation Discovery. Occasionally, she takes a break to write books and test the limits of her mind. Also an avid horror movie fan, she likes to incorporate dark elements into the majority of her books.

View Yolanda's books by scanning here;